Night Hungers

Aarons Kiss Series Book 10

By

Kathi S. Barton

World Castle Publishing

Kathi S. Barton

World Castle Publishing
Pensacola, Florida

Copyright © Kathi S. Barton 2012
ISBN: 9781938961427
First Edition World Castle Publishing November 1, 2012
http://www.worldcastlepublishing.com

Licensing Notes

Cover: Karen Fuller
Photos: Shutterstock
Editor: Brieanna Robertson

Kathi S. Barton

CHAPTER 1

"Zane? Come out from under there a minute. I got a customer that has a question for you. I don't think the idiot has a clue what he's talking about."

Allison Zander rolled the creeper out from the car she was working on and glared up at her boss Danny March. He was the nicest man she knew. And most of the time she wanted to smack him because he was very overprotective of her and very chauvinistic as well. But she needed the job and he needed her help. The man was a complete novice on the newer engines and Zane wasn't.

"What's he saying? If it's that moron from the police garage again I swear I'll quit if you make me talk to him. I can't understand a word he's saying when he gets all romantic. Never seen a man who drools as much as that one."

"Nah. It's that guy from the city garage. He says that you pulled his crankshaft too tight and he wants a refund. I can't even find his record that we even worked on his car. He said you were going to do it on the side."

Zane rolled back under the car she was working on before Danny could see her blush. That was another thing about him. He just didn't get innuendos or double-entendres.

"Danny, he thinks that I should give him a blow job because I turned him down the other night when he cornered me at the grocery store. He's telling you that he has a hard-on and that I'm a prick tease."

Zane could feel his anger, but she had to hand it to him, he didn't move to the man. Not yet at any rate. She watched as he bounced on his feet, toes to heel, toes to heel.

"And the refund? What is that supposed to mean? That he's giving you another chance to loosen his crankshaft? Mother flower pots, Zane, how do you know this stuff?"

"He told me. Danny, whatever you're thinking of doing, don't. He isn't worth it. Just give me a—fuck! Danny, come back here."

Zane rolled from under the car and snatched up the first tool she could lay her hands on. It just happened to be an eighteen inch monkey wrench. She came to the front of the shop just in time to see the man, Carl...somebody backing away from Danny. Danny had a crescent wrench only marginally smaller than hers. She came up behind her boss, stepped just to the right of him, and faced Carl.

"Danny, sir, please don't kill him like you did the other man. You know that somebody is gonna miss them one of these days and I don't know what I'd do without your protection."

Danny "the killer" turned, looked at her, and raised his brow. She knew she sounded helpless and hoped that he'd play along. She winked back at him and smiled. Then she simpered a little and wiped at a nonexistent tear.

"You know how I hate it when men hit on you. Just let me do this one in and I promise the next...the next five I'll let go with a warning. I'll even let you decide if he goes fast or slow."

"Now see here. I don't want any trouble. She came on to me. I was with my family when she...why, she propositioned me. Right there in the Shop a Lot parking lot. I nearly had to call the police when—"

"Don't hang yourself, buddy. Get the heck out of here and don't even stop by here for gas. I have a good memory for butt wipes and you've hit the top of my nasty list. And leave Zane alone."

When the guy got back in his car and peeled out of the lot Zane and Danny burst out laughing. They were still laughing when Zane rolled under the car again and started working on the muffler. Danny started closing down the shop.

"Why don't you come over for dinner tonight? Russell is making his famous beef stroganoff and homemade noodles. I think I might even have a bottle of the red wine you like so much. I think I got the right one this time."

Zane knew it wasn't going to be the right wine. For one thing, it wasn't sold in stores and for another, it wasn't wine but blood. She had been drinking blood when he found her having a sip. It's not as though she needed blood all the time, she wasn't a vamp or anything. But it did help her heal and keep her strong. Her powers were strong and she had a great deal of them, but they did take a lot of her energy and she could get hurt when down like that.

Zane was sure that Danny knew she wasn't human, but he'd never asked her. It was as if it were an unspoken trust between them. She knew that most of his customers weren't human either, most of them being weres with a few vampires and fairies thrown into the mix. Danny was a great guy, honest and without a single prejudiced bone in his body.

"Sure. But no veggies. I hate those suckers and I won't have you trying to dress them up as something like a salad or anything. The first sign of green, leafy, or sprouty on my plate and I'm so out of there. Deal?"

"Sure, Miss Carnivore. But will it be all right if Russell and I have a salad or a green bean? *We* like our vegetables. It balances out our menu. I'll see you at six. Don't be late."

Zane finished clamping the muffler onto the chassie and then gathered up her tools. She loved them and the way they fit into her hand, what she could do with them, and how they were put together. Every night before she left she wiped them down and put them in the drawer that was lined in foam and had cut-outs for each one. She was as meticulous with her tools as she was with everything else she owned—cautious, precise, and deliberate. At twenty after five, ten minutes after Danny locked up, Zane was moving to the back of the shop and shifting as she went.

~~~

"So...you gonna ask her tonight? She's been coming here enough and she has to know that we've guessed some of it. And I don't know about you, but I'm really curious as to what she is."

Danny was helping Russell fix the salad he had told Zane they were having. Russell was right and they had had this discussion before. Every time Zane came over to their house they would ponder what she was. It didn't really matter to either of them, but they were wondering more and more.

Like today. Danny had hoped she'd just tell him what she was drinking and not let him go on about finding the right brand. He knew that wine hadn't been what she'd been drinking that day. He knew enough vamps to know blood when he smelled it. But she didn't only drink it. She ate real food too. Plus, she worked during the day for them. Then there was the fact that he'd never seen her wear a coat. Danny knew a lot of werewolves and they ran hot-blooded too. That really didn't mean anything, but it still was something to think about.

"Yeah, I'm thinking about it. But we have to ease into it slowly. I don't want to freak her out if she's nothing more than she seems on the outside. I really like her and I don't want her to run off because we insulted her."

When the doorbell rang five minutes later, at six on the dot, Danny went to let their guest in. As usual, she was dressed in black from head to toe. He smiled when she handed him a bunch of wildflowers, Russell's favorite.

She was a very beautiful woman. She was as tall as he was at six foot. Zane seldom wore her hair down, but the one time he'd seen it, he knew that it was straight and thick. As black as the night, it looked almost blue under certain light and hung well past her hips. Her eyes were dark; he'd never been able to figure out if they were dark brown or just black. Their color seemed to change with her mood. The deeper her emotion, the darker they appeared. Her pale skin was flawless, and across her nose was a sprinkle of maybe a dozen or so freckles. Her lips were full and as pouty as he'd ever seen and made a man, even a gay man like him, think of deep kisses under the moon and sex. Danny knew that she was large busted. She wore a t-shirt—black again—in the shop and it fit her very well. He'd never seen her in anything but black leather pants and they left no doubt that Zane was a well formed, well turned woman.

"Everything smells good. I found those outside of where I'm staying. Thought Russell might like them," she said as she moved toward the kitchen.

"He will. I think he would like to learn the names of them so that he can start his own garden in the back. I don't suppose you know the names of these, do you?"

That was another thing about Zane that made them curious about her. She knew a little something about everything. Danny had always liked that she never made him feel stupid when he talked to her either.

"Sure. I can write them out for you guys. Hello, Russell. Dinner smells good. If you put any of the green crap on my plate, I'm going to be really pissy."

Zane kissed Russell on the cheek and settled down on one of the bar stools. Danny set the flowers on the counter and pulled a vase out from under the sink. He would just drop them in the thing and then set them on the table knowing that Russell would bring them back into the kitchen and rearrange them. It was a game they played.

In no time they were sitting at the dining room table and eating. When Russell passed Zane the salad bowl she simply set it on the floor and shoved it under the chair with her foot. Danny retrieved the bowl and set it closer to him. The next move on both their parts was to start throwing bits of it at each other and he didn't want to have to clean lettuce out of the curtains again.

"Danny was telling me that he had to save you from having to adjust some man's crankshaft tonight. I wish I could have seen you acting all girly. I bet that was a sight to see." Russell kicked him under the table. He was hinting, and not so surreptitiously, that he was opening the door for him.

Danny rolled his eyes and pulled his feet further under his chair. "Zane, Russell and I really enjoy your company. And we like you, so if we get too personal or go too far, let us know. But we wanted to ask you something."

"I'm not having your baby," Zane said with a grin. "I like you guys too, but I draw the line at carrying around a ton of weight out of friendship. Anything else, well, we can discuss that too."

"What Danny is trying to say is we'd like to know what you are. You're a woman, we get that, but what species are you? And like he said, we're not trying to hurt you about this."

Zane stared at Russell then looked at Danny. He would have preferred that they worked up to this a little slower, but Russell had never been known for his patience. Danny was ready to tell her to forget it when she answered.

"I'm not really sure they named what I am. I'm a test tube anomaly that was created by mixing the DNA from several species. And I'm not easily offended."

"You drink blood. I mean, the wine, it was blood. Do you have fangs? Can you bite people?" Danny felt stupid for blurting it out like that as soon as the words spilled from his lips.

"Yes. I drink blood on occasion. When I'm hurt or drained of energy, I need to drink it. And yes, I have fangs to drink from someone if I need to. I don't often, but there have been times when it was necessary. I don't need it like a vampire does, but I do need it. I feed about twice a week, more if I'm injured."

Zane leaned down to pick up Russell's cat and Danny thought of something else. He'd wanted to ask about her tattoos for a long time and since she was willing to answer, he thought he'd find out. He just hoped the answer wasn't as scary as he thought it might be.

"You have tattoos on your back and arms. They're very detailed and...well, they're very unusual. Not just for a woman, but unusual for tats. Do they have anything to do with what you are?"

Instead of answering him she stood up, pulled her t-shirt up over her back, and turned her back to them. With her shirt over her shoulders, he and Russell could see the sword in a scabbard tattooed in the center of her back along her spine.

The detail was exquisite, the colors brilliant and bright. The scabbard reached from her scapulas to the bottom of her spine at about twelve inches and was at the widest place about six inches. It was bejeweled with what appeared to be gemstones and diamonds. The handle of the sword was covered in a cuff that was intricate and practical.

"Could you pick up Lovely? When I show you this she will be scared. The force of energy when I do this is a bit...well, it's a bit overwhelming."

Russell picked up his cat and held her to his chest. Danny wished he had something to hold too. Because when Zane reached back with her left hand and touched the handle of the blade, it peeled from her skin and filled her hand. As they watched the blade pulled from the scabbard and became as real as the silverware on the table. And when she turned with the blade in her hand, he knew what color her eyes were. They were black, black as sin.

CHAPTER 2

Zane laid her sword on the table in front of the two men. Neither of them said a word, but she could feel their fear and their confusion. Maybe she should have told them what was going to happen before she showed them, but she didn't think they'd believe her.

The sword was just as it looked on her back. The cuff was made of silver and curved around her hand perfectly. It would never fit another person's hand, as she was the only one who could remove it from her back. And if she was injured and rendered unconscious it would return to her back and look for all anyone could tell as a simple tat.

"I don't want you two to freak out on me. If you think you can handle any more, or even if you want any more, I can tell you. I trust you not to tell anyone."

It seemed to take a great deal of effort for them to tear their eyes away from the blade lying on the table. Danny looked at her first. His eyes were full of questions and she was sure his mind, if she looked, would be close to overloaded.

"There's more? Holy pod puckers, Zane. I thought you'd...I just wanted to know about the tat. I didn't...I never thought that...mother flower pots, that's messed up. Give me a minute."

Zane stood, picked up the blade, and returned it to her back. She was walking to the door when Danny jumped up. She didn't even slow her stride. She needed to get out of there now.

"Zane, please don't—"

"It's all right, Danny. I understand completely. I have to go anyway. There are some things I have to do before tomorrow. I'll see you at the shop then?"

If she was out of work she'd simply move on. She'd done it before and she had no doubt that she'd have to do it again and again. This was the first time she'd ever shown anyone what she could do and she thought it would more than likely be the last.

"Of course. Zane, I'm sorry. It was just...it was just a shock. Russell and I knew that you were different, but we never dreamed that you were anything, that you could do anything like we just witnessed."

"I'll see you. Good night then. And tell Russell that I said dinner was great. I'll see you tomorrow, Danny."

She moved to the end of his lot and shifted. She needed a good, hard run and figured that she'd sneak onto the pack property, again, that the wolves ran on. She'd see if she could find a few of them out running. Weres were not very tolerant of shifters in general, but they had never figured she was anything but a stray wolf, she thought. It took her twenty minutes to navigate through the street and keep out of sight, and another ten to find a group of four young pups to run with. She was just getting back to her lair when the sun was coming up. After a short nap of an hour she was headed back to the garage to pull an engine.

At noon she was buried deep under the hood of an SUV that the owner had never had serviced when Danny came back. He had talked to her off and on all morning, but neither of them had mentioned last night. She didn't like it and figured if things between them didn't improve by the next week she would move on. She liked Danny too much to make him this uncomfortable.

"Do you think you can look at another SUV for me? This guy is a good friend and he claims that it's making a strange noise. Duncan is very...well, very proper, but one of the nicest, if not strangest, men you'll ever meet. You'll like him."

"Sure. This one is going to need a whole new engine. It's seized up from lack of oil. Why would someone pay this much for one of these suckers and not keep it up? Damned shame. You can

14

bring Duncan through here and I'll roll this oversized paperweight out to the back. I'll have the estimate done on it when I look at this car."

Danny nodded and moved back to the front. Zane opened the back bay doors, put the piece of crap into neutral, and gave it a small push to get it rolling. If she were the owner she'd just let it keep rolling until it was out of sight. When it came to a stop at the very edge of the lot she put it back into park and closed and locked it up. The guy was going to be pissed about it being out in the sun, but at this point it didn't matter.

The dark green SUV was being rolled into the bay slot just as Zane was coming back through the main door. The little man behind the wheel looked to be both nervous and terrified at the same time. Zane looked behind her to see if something came in behind her. When he got out and walked around the vehicle she realized he had been afraid of hitting something in the garage.

"Duncan, this is Allison Zander; Zane, this is Duncan. He works at the MacManus household as the man of everything. Duncan, why don't you tell Zane what you told me that your car is doing."

"It is pulling very hard to the left. When I try to keep it straight it makes a funny screeching noise. Not unlike Miss Lizzy does when she is told that she must retire for the evening. I do hope that it is easy to fix. I must pick up the children at their school at precisely two-fifteen."

Zane glanced at Danny. *Seriously?* Shrugging to herself, Zane asked him for the keys. When he handed them to her she hopped into the car and started it up.

"I'll need to take it for a spin. I should be back in about ten minutes. I promise nothing will happen to it."

When he looked at Danny then back at her and nodded, Zane pulled the door shut and backed out. She thought it was just out of alignment, but wanted to be sure it was nothing more. Turning left out of the lot, she drove down to the first stop sign then turned in the empty bar lot down the street and headed back. Yeah, it was out of alignment. When she got back to the garage Duncan was on his cell phone so she pulled the car up onto the lifts and began to raise it up. When he walked over to her with his phone still out she looked at him.

"Her ladyship would like a word with you, if you please. She is most concerned about the children, you see, and if I will be able to pick them up. I have told her your name."

Zane took the proffered cell phone and put it to her ear as the car came to a rest just above her head. She walked under the vehicle just as she answered the phone. It was noisy in the garage so she had to ask "her ladyship" twice to repeat what she said.

"I said that if Duncan needs to have a ride back home I can pick him up after I get the kids from school. Don't you have an office or something that isn't quite so noisy? I know Danny very well and I'm sure that he wouldn't mind you using it to talk to customers."

"That would defeat the point of *him* having an office if everyone could just use it whenever the mood struck, don't you think? I'll need to do an alignment on this and I should have it ready by seven. You'll have to talk to Danny about picking it up after hours. When he leaves, he locks up and I don't do the business part of helping him."

"I'll talk to him. If you wouldn't mind telling Duncan that I'll pick him up around three I'd appreciate it. Also, if you could have Danny call me, that would be very helpful."

Zane wanted to tell her that she wasn't the frigging secretary, that she could call Danny herself, but she just said sure and hung up. Zane was pulling the air gun over just as Duncan wandered over to her and stood behind her. She didn't mind so much him watching, it was how intently he did so. Like there was going to be a test at the end and he needed to make a good grade. When she had to move him twice to finish taking off the tire Duncan sat down at the work bench. Thirty minutes into the job he asked her a question.

"I was wondering, Miss Zander, if you could tell me who this book belongs to. I was not even aware that you could find *King*

Lear in Latin. I would love to borrow it sometime if I could ask the owner."

Zane glanced over at the book in question. It was hers and she had nearly finished it. She didn't own any books. This one she had just picked up at a used bookstore in the Short North a few days ago. One of the many things that Zane could do was memorize things and, once read, she didn't need to re-read it to know what each page had on it.

"I should have it finished tomorrow. If you really want it I'll leave it in your vehicle when you pick it up. I just finished Poe's *The Raven* in Latin if you want it. You should be able to find it in the second drawer of that cabinet by your leg."

"Splendid! I shall read this one then and return it to you posthaste. If you could tell me what price you paid for this I will gladly pay you for its usage. I cannot find books in this language in the local library and will find this to be a very nice treat for me."

Zane put her tool cart closer to her and continued to work while she talked to the man. Switching to Latin she began talking to him about the few books she had read over the past several months and where she had found them. The time flew by both because she was busy and because she was really enjoying the conversation and the man. Soon Danny was yelling to the back that Duncan's ride was here.

"Thank you for the book, Miss Zander. I will enjoy reading it and think of you when I do so. I look forward to continuing our conversation at some later date perhaps."

"Sure, and it's just Zane. Not Miss anything. I'll leave *Lear* in the car for you. Like I said, pass it on if you want or sell it in a garage sale. And thank you for an enjoyable afternoon."

At seven-thirty Zane was just finishing up tightening the bolts on the SUV. She was tired, having not gotten a great deal of sleep the night before, and ready to lie down. Moving toward the door, her pager went off. Not even bothering to look at the display, she went to the payphone just outside of Danny's office and called the number she knew by heart.

"I have a job for you. There's a rogue werewolf outside of Cincinnati that needs to be destroyed. Can you do it for us by the weekend? The job is sanctioned."

Zane had never met the voice at the other end. She didn't really care who it was so long as they continued to pay her well and keep her secret. She was sure the man was in an office somewhere sitting his huge, fat butt behind a desk and waiting for someone to screw up so that she could go out and clean up. Working for this person had kept her from putting a bullet to her head, not that it would do any more than make her weak.

"Yeah. I can do it. I'll pick the stuff up tonight if that's okay. I have to be somewhere in the morning, but I can have it done by late tomorrow night."

"Good. I will make sure that everything you need is there. Box number twelve. Good night, Mac."

It took Zane less than a minute to shift and to arrive at the little apartment building on Tenth Avenue. She pulled the large envelope out of mailbox twelve marked with her cover name *Mechanic* on it. Stuffing it under her t-shirt and next to her skin, Zane shifted and left the area. It wasn't until she was in her lair that she opened it. Reading the information and then burning the envelope's contents, she lay down and promptly fell asleep.

~~~

"So how long can you stay? I'm hoping you'll say forever, but I guess that's too much to hope for. I miss my baby brother."

Aiden St. James just smiled. He did want to stay in the United States. France had become rather stale without Tristan there to have fun with and Aiden and his other two brothers had nothing in common any more. Finding their mates had made them sort of boring, Aiden thought.

"Baby brother? Trist, I'm nearly six hundred years old. Don't you think it's about time you dropped the baby crap? And where is my favorite niece? Surely this vision can't be her."

Emma came running at him full tilt. She really was a vision, too. Blond curly hair, fair skin—she was going to be a killer when she got a little older. He couldn't wait to watch Tristan try and deal with her dating. Scooping the little girl up in his arms, Aiden leaned down and kissed his sister-in-law Bailey on the cheek. A low growl from Tristan made him laugh.

"Oh behave, you overgrown baby. It's your brother. If anyone is allowed to kiss my cheek, it's him. How are you, Aiden? Did he even ask you to sit down before he started browbeating you into moving here?"

"No. He barely let me take my shoes off before he started hounding me about it. I swear, Bailey, how you put up with him is beyond me. Maybe you and Miss Emma here should come and stay with me. I'm sure I could make you very happy."

Bailey laughed when Aiden wiggled his brows at her. Another growl from Tristan had them both roaring with laughter. As they moved to the living room out of the main hall Aiden talked to Emma.

"I brought you some things from your Grandma and Grandpa St. James. They also told me to tell you that they'll be here next month and that you were to make a list of things you'd like to show them when they visit. I thought I was going to be bringing them this time, but something came up at the office at the last minute so they had to stay."

Aiden heard the, "I'll just bet it did" from Tristan and grinned at him. It had taken a lot of planning to make the last minute thing happen just as he was leaving for the airport and it almost wasn't enough to make them stay. But in the end, he'd won. He wanted this trip to be about seeing if he could make it work here rather than about having to be a third wheel in entertaining his parents. He loved them dearly, but a man needed some time with his brother.

"Did you bring me anything, Uncle Aiden? I loved the horsey you sent me, but Momma said I can't ride it. I think the pretty colors are so beautiful."

Emma said beautiful as if it were a long three syllable word, enunciating each one like she meant them. He loved this little girl and was very glad that Bailey and Tristan had adopted her.

Bailey couldn't have children. She had been engineered in a lab and was trained as a killer. But when she and a few others had been slated to be destroyed Bailey and four others decided that the corporation, Co-Tech Industries, had to go.

"No, you can't ride it. But I think I might have been able to find a pretty unicorn for you that matches your horsey. I have to make sure that it's not a fake before I send it to you."

"Oh! I seen a unicorn at Aunt Mel's castle. She was so pretty and she let me touch her. I had to be really, really, really careful or she would be skirty. Momma said that only special people get to see them 'cause nobody believes in them no more. Why is that, Uncle Aiden? They sure could make the world so pretty if they were to come here, don't you think?"

"Everything is 'pretty' now," Bailey told him. "Last month everything was 'lovely.' It depends on what new word she hears that she repeats all the time. I shudder to think what she might hear next. Come along, sweetheart, it's bedtime."

"Ah, I see. And 'skirty?' I take that to mean 'skittish?'"

"Yes. Very good. I have to get her to bed. If I don't, she'll be a terror in the morning. And I need my quiet time more and more lately. Tell Uncle Aiden goodnight, baby."

He kissed Emma's forehead and handed her back to her mother. Bailey took her up the stairs and disappeared around the corner. Aiden went to the study with his brother.

CHAPTER 3

Zane watched her target move along the building. She'd been following him for the past hour and he never seemed to be alone. If he didn't move to a quieter place, and alone, she was going to have to change her plans and shoot him. That would not only be messy, but also dangerous.

Just as she was about to move in for the shot he moved to the front of the abandoned building and slipped inside. Zane wasn't sure what was in the large warehouse, but she was willing to bet whatever it was couldn't be good. The file she had on him said that he was dealing in making and disturbing rock cocaine. She was afraid that's what this was going to be.

As soon as he shut the door behind him Zane moved closer. By the time she was slipping into the door five minutes had passed. It didn't take her long to find his scent and that of the projects he had going on within the building. Not only was her target making crack, he was also dealing in meth. She moved back to the front of the building and reached out to her contact with the cell phone that had been in the second envelope that had arrived at her work early this morning.

"There's a problem. I've found his money-making projects and he's in the building. If I blow it like I should, it's going to be cleaner. If I call the cops to find it, I'm not hanging around to make sure he gets dead. Up to you."

"Blow it. Make sure there is the least amount of casualties as possible without causing an issue. I'll leave the way you do it in your hands. I can extend your time to Saturday if you wish. The client will be pleased about the drugs. What are they, by the way?"

"Yeah, I'll need the extra day to get the place set up. The coke is here that you said and meth. From the smell I'd say he has a large set up going. I can make it look like an accident from the heat. I'll leave enough evidence so the cops don't worry what happened."

"Very well. Saturday then. Good luck and be safe, Mechanic," he said. Then the phone went dead.

Zane took out the battery of the phone and held it in her hand. Pouring energy into it, she dropped it as soon as it flared with heat. Anyone who picked it up would never know it had been a battery at one time. She did the same with the phone itself. She'd been working with this man long enough to know he'd never used the same phone twice. And she destroyed it so that no one would ever be able to track it her back to her.

Moving deep into the belly of the building again, she followed her nose to get to the lab. She was surprised at how massive the operation was. Not only did he have several hundred different heat stations, he also had an assembly line of workers filling the containers for distribution. It was both disturbing and fascinating to her that he'd never been caught.

Zane stayed in the building until she noticed that at around midnight people started cleaning up their stations and were getting ready to leave. Her target had never ventured from his office in the four hours she'd been there. She knew that he was above the work area, so she knew that he was still close. Doing a mental scan of the building she knew that, other than her target, there were two men in the room with him. Everyone else had left.

Moving to the floor were the workers had been Zane started lighting small fires among the areas just far enough away from the highly volatile drugs. She figured she had approximately ten minutes to make sure that her target would be found in part of the carnage. When she was satisfied that it would soon be burning out of control Zane went to the door of his office.

She never got the name of the targets she was to take out. Not that she felt she'd make some sort of personal attachments to them. She just didn't want to have to deal with more things in her mind to remember. Some days it was hard enough trying not to remember some of the things she'd done. She didn't want to think about having names to try not to think about too. Pressing both hands to the oak door Zane listened to the conversation going on inside.

"I think we should buy the building and be done with it. There are a couple bigger ones, but this one is just far enough off the beaten path to afford us all the privacy we want. Besides, we can get it cheaper because of where it's located."

"Yes. But what happens when we expand? You know as well as I do that the only reason we haven't gotten caught is because we pay so well. If we have to hire more and more workers, who's to say they wouldn't turn us in just for the thrill of it? I just think we should hold off for another couple of months."

The man who had spoken last was her target. A quick touch of his mind told her that. The other man, the one who had spoken first, was none other than the assistant chief of police. That was just great. The third man was a were. Zane slipped inside his mind quickly then back out. Now she had a problem. He was DEA and he was working to bring these two to justice. She did the only thing she could do with...three minutes to go.

"I need you to get out of the building. It's going to blow very soon now, in about three minutes, as a matter of fact."

"Who is this? I've been working this case for nearly three months. I swear to Christ if you fuck this up for me, I'll hunt you down." The man was pissed. Not that Zane could blame him, but still.

"I'm coming in so you need to tell me where you are so that I don't accidently hurt you. I've been ordered to kill the wolf by someone of higher authority than you."

"Fuck you. You come through that door and I'll shoot you. I don't care who you think is your higher authority. My gun says I win." Zane felt his anger as he spoke.

She debated for all of one second. He'd been warned. If something happened to him then so be it. Least amount of causalities possible was her orders. It mattered little to her if he didn't want to help her not kill him. Reaching into the room she could tell where each person was; the wolf she needed was directly in front of her. She could feel movement of someone and, with a quick dip into the mind, she knew she'd found her DEA agent. Gathering power from around her Zane exploded the door off its hinges and into the room. A blast of power to the target then another to the police officer killed them where they sat. She turned to the agent just before he fired at her. Quickness on her part is all that saved her from a fatal shot to the head. The agent was dead before the room exploded beneath her.

~~~

Aiden was standing at the bar at Blood Moon when his brother and Aaron showed up. Tristan was dressed in his usual button down dress shirt, tie, suit coat, and brogans. Aaron, however, was dressed as every cliché vampire Aiden had ever read about. Dark pants, dark silk shirt, and long dark hair that he'd tied back with a leather tie. Aiden was sure he was projecting an image, he was part owner of the bar, but it was still funny to him.

"I thought you old men would be a little longer." Aiden looked at his brother and the others as he spoke. "I just asked about a donor here. Why don't I meet you guys in the back later?"

Tristan had told Aiden yesterday that the bar had originally been set up to be for the paranormal, but their attorney had pointed out how that wouldn't work and now there were humans wandering around. But there was a way for vamps to feed from willing humans and weres alike.

"Go ahead. The ladies are still shopping and we have plenty of time. And Bradley called to say he was going to be late. Something about a shifter on his land without permission."

Aiden only half listened to his brother. He was watching the woman come toward him. A fairy. Vampires couldn't get drunk, drugs didn't affect them, and they couldn't get any sexually transmitted diseases. But fairy blood could make all those vises seem like child's play when drank, but only if one had permission. Without it, the blood was poison.

Taking the woman, Scalar, to the back room, he leaned her against the wall and inhaled her scent. Clean and fresh, but not who he wanted. Licking her pulse, Scalar put her hands around his waist and moved closer to him, her body molding to his.

"Sorry, darling, I just want dinner. I'm supposed to be meeting my family right now and there isn't time for that. I have to say it's hard, very hard, to turn such a luscious creature down, but I like to take my time when I have sex."

"Are you sure? You're very hard and I could really use a good fuck. Please?" she begged prettily.

Aiden ran his tongue down her throat again. "Sorry, sweetheart, but I can make it good for you. Close your eyes and think of me. That's it, think of my cock deep inside of you."

Planting the images of them having sex was easy. He was a little disconcerted that she had thought his cock was so small, but he needed to feed before too much more time passed. He was fairly old and a pureblood, being born a vampire instead of turned, so he didn't need to feed often. But he'd been putting it off more and more and he was going to get himself into trouble soon if he didn't get better at it. Sighing deeply, he nudged Scalar to her release and bit her. Hot blood filled his mouth and slid down his throat. When her climax was coming to an end Aiden pushed her again as he sealed the tiny prick marks at her neck. She would be weak for a little while, but more than likely blame that on two really hard climaxes. Once he tipped her he walked out the back door to get a breath of fresh warm air.

Aiden had four brothers who had all found their mates. He was the baby of the family and the only one who'd not found his mate. He wanted to find her, wanted to spend the rest of his days making her happy, pleasing her, but mostly he wanted someone he could be with. Even with his family, all of them, Aiden was still lonely.

Going back inside, he moved to the back where everyone was. He sat down next to his brother and was able to move right into the conversation. It seemed that Bradley was still going on about the shifter on his land.

"It's a female. I don't know why the pups didn't recognize her scent. I certainly did, it was all over them. They said that they'd played with her before. And that she was really fun. Fun? What the fuck does that mean? Fun my ass. She was trespassing, trespassing on my land."

"What are you going to do? I mean, with that much land you certainly can't watch the whole thing. And as for the pups, can't really blame them. A female out for a run, maybe they didn't tell you because they were learning the ways around her. You know, getting a little tail." Kyle was the only one that laughed at his own joke. Aiden smiled, but knew that it was a little too tense for his taste around the table.

"That's just it, they said that she wasn't there but to play. They actually thought she was a full blood. The only reason I know she wasn't is because her scent was a little too perfect, too clean on them. And there was the magic. I could smell it on them."

They spent another three hours sitting around talking. They were all good friends and by the time they left Aiden felt like he was with old friends and good ones.

CHAPTER 4

Zane was under a car when Danny came back to the bay area three days later. They had been dancing around each other, not saying anything, yet talking a lot. When he said her name she didn't even come out from under the car but continued to work.

"Zane, Duncan called. He wants to know if you want a few books he picked up on the Internet. He said to have you call him when you get a chance. He's also bringing in a couple of other cars to be serviced."

Zane had just finished reading something she'd picked up over the weekend and was ready for something new. "Yeah, I'll call him, thanks."

Danny didn't move away from the car. She could still see his feet from where she was. He was doing that toe to heel thing again and she wanted to tell him to go away, but it was his shop.

"Russell said that we may have...that we may have been a little rude to you the other day. I wanted to tell you, that is, we wanted to...fuck, Zane, I'm sorry. It's just that neither of us had seen anything like that before. I...we want you to come over tonight and talk to us. Okay?"

Zane took a deep breath and smiled. Danny was still freaked out, she could even smell his fear, but he was willing to let that go. She was just about to tell him she'd love to come to dinner when her pager went off at her waist.

"I'm sorry, Danny, but I have something to do tonight. How about Friday night again? I might even be persuaded to eat a leaf or something. That is, if it's okay with you two."

"Sure. Great. Friday night it is then. I'll make you a steak and you don't have to eat anything that will be healthy. I'll even have a pack of blood for you on hand if you want. I know this vamp that can get it for us."

She grinned again. "That won't be necessary. I'll just drain a bad guy or two before I come over." When he didn't move, not even to rock, she laughed. "I'm kidding, Danny. I'll be there, and don't worry about the blood. I only need it if I'm hurt."

As soon as he left she got up and went to the payphone. Dialing in, she called her contact. Twice in one week was unusual for him and she was surprised to hear from him.

"I have a shifter in your immediate area that's kidnapped a vampire. The vampire is from another realm and needs to be returned posthaste. I will send the information to post office box fifteen. Questions?"

"Shifter? What's the animal of choice, do you know?" Zane's was a panther, black, sleek, and huge. She used that animal more than anything.

"Eagle. Although, you should know that this shifter can also change its sex at will. The change is almost undetectable. I have sent a small vial of blood and an article of clothing for you."

Zane could do that as well, though she didn't unless it was an emergency. It was hard to do and required a great deal of energy. Plus, she didn't particularly know much about the opposite sex, so she was always afraid she'd mess up with some male thing and not know it until it was too late.

After finishing up for the day, she cleaned up her tools and put them away. She thought about the vampire she was supposed to retrieve and wondered if he was injured. They could be quite mean when they were hungry and she didn't want to have to kill him as soon as she recovered him. Her blood, like fairy blood, was poisonous when taken without permission.

Shifting into the panther, she made her way to the apartment complex on Eighteenth Street and got the mail out of the box. There were drops all over the state that they used, mostly in rundown neighborhoods and not anywhere there were cameras. Putting the package close to her skin, she moved out into the street and shifted just on the other side of the city limits. When she was well away from the prying eyes of anyone around she pulled out the large envelope.

Inside were three sealed bags. One contained a vial with what looked like blood; the other two had strips of cloth marked with the words "shifter" and "vampire." There was also a file and a few photos of the vampire. None of the kidnapper. And a pay-as-you-go cell phone. Putting the phone inside of her black tee, she opened the first baggie. The scent of the vamp was strong; blood permeated the bag and the blue silk. The other baggie, the scent was faint, but strong enough for her to get a trail for the search. It took her one more minute to figure out how to scent the blood—taste or smell. She went for smell. And what she had been afraid of happened. There wasn't anything to scent and she had to taste. Vile, evil blood touched her tongue. A strong enough scent that she could now follow the shifter anywhere, at any distance; it was just a matter of time that she caught up with it. She shifted again. It took her eleven minutes to get to the end of the trail.

The cave where the two of them were was high, it's opening narrow that would have been difficult to find without the scent to follow. Moving upwind she got as close as she could to the opening and waited. Closing her eyes, the panther looked to be as much a part of the blackening night as the green of the grass. Zane reached, she reached deep into the cavern and found them to be on one of the lower levels of the cave. The vamp was badly injured and he was in the sleep of his kind, probably to conserve energy. Good, he wouldn't be in the way trying to help her. The shifter, male, was sitting next to heat and not moving. Shifting into a small insect, Zane moved inside.

Landing on the ceiling of the cave just above the shifter, Zane looked around. There wasn't really that much to see, just a bunch of stone and a small natural pond next to the shifter. The vamp was about ten feet from him and he was lying very still. Zane couldn't detect any heartbeat or any breaths. Moving into his mind she could tell that he was in a sleep still and not yet dead, though he needed blood and very soon.

There was a fire in a circle of stones that had to have been the source of heat she had felt. The shifter sat on another stone and was writing in a notebook. He looked to be working very hard at something. Dropping silently to the ground, she shifted again, this time into her human self. He turned when she stood up.

They stared at one another for several seconds. When he stood up and turned to her he started to pull something from behind him.

"I wouldn't do that. I'm much faster than you can be and bullets won't kill me. Just give me the vamp and I'll be on my way."

He laughed at her and brought his gun forward. Even from here she could see that it was a smaller Glock. It wasn't loaded with silver, that much she could smell, but it did have a silencer. Who needed a silencer in a cave, she wondered?

"Are you faster than a bullet? I don't think so. And the vamp? He's going to bring me a great deal of money. I was just writing his ransom note now. He's a big deal in the Council. If you're really nice I'll let you be my partner."

Zane didn't move, but she did put her hands on her thighs, closing her hands over the tattoos there. She waited. Watching him, she knew the exact moment that he was going to pull the trigger. Before she moved the vamp woke and made a noise.

The shifter moved the gun toward the vamp and Zane jumped. The bullet hit her hard and knocked her back against the wall. Pulling out the guns, hers loaded with silver, she shot the shifter eight times in the chest and six more in the head. Taking a deep breath and pushing the pain as far away from her as she could, Zane stood up and moved to the body. Reaching behind her and pulling out the blade she removed his head. Pulling energy from the earth and the air she threw it into the body and head of the sifter. It exploded ash and dried bone settled down around the fire and ground.

The vamp was still out. But she knew in her present condition, a bullet in her side, she had to get him to safety. Unknown to the person who hired her she could smell another shifter in the area. Zane sat on the rock where the shifter had been writing, picked up his notebook, and read what he'd been working on.

"Mastir Vampyre, McManus,

I want sevin million dollors for the vampyre I have kiddnnapped. He is very fameous and he is worth it. I will not kilt him if you pay me. We can"

Brilliant this guy had not been. But she did have a name. Pulling out the cell phone, she dialed the only number in it. Without much in the way of greeting, she launched into her problems.

"The shifter is dead, but he had a partner. I have the vamp, but he needs feed. I've been injured and can't feed him. There's a Master McManus that the shifter was going to ransom the vamp to. Do you know who he is and if he can help this guy out?"

"Yes. His name is MacManus and I know him. Hold on." Zane looked down at the wound. It was still bleeding badly. When the man came back on the line Zane was wondering if she could feed too. "He is at the Blood Moon. A bar in the Merchant District. I cannot contact him, but he will help you."

Zane hung up when he did. She knew where the bar was; she'd been there once. The problem was, she was bleeding and going to a vampire bar. Closing her eyes, she laid her hand over the wound and covered it with deep magic. She couldn't heal herself without making it worse, but she could cover it. After making sure the vamp was all right, she shifted and made her way to the bar.

By the time she was walking to the front door she knew that she should have fed first. Her body was weakening. Not to the point of being dangerous, but she was nervous about being weak and meeting with a master vampire. She knew nothing about him other than a few snippets of information she'd heard around the garage.

Inside, she could smell the blood. It was rich and strong and the pulsing hearts were making her dizzy. She moved across the floor, ignoring everything but keeping herself under control when she heard a shout. Looking up, she saw a man coming at her quickly. A wolf. Alpha wolf. And he was not a happy camper. And neither were the five men that were coming along with him. When she was grabbed from either side by the other men she shifted.

Her panther slid from the grips of the men holding her and she leapt up on the bar. Two seconds had passed since the alpha had charged at her. It took her another two to figure out which of the men would be the most dangerous to her.

Leaping toward him, both front feet hit him in the chest, knocking him and her to the floor. As she landed next to him, she clamped her powerful jaws around his throat and bit down, not breaking skin—not yet at any rate.

CHAPTER 5

Aiden didn't move. Not that he could with her teeth at his jugular. His chest hurt and he was sure that he could feel two, maybe three, broken ribs. He wasn't worried about the injuries; he was already healing from those. But if she ripped his throat out, there would be no coming back from that.

"Aiden, can you knock her off? I can't kill her with her on top of you like that."

Her teeth dug deeper into his skin and he could feel a drop of blood pearl on his skin then her hot tongue swiping at it.

"I think she can fucking understand you, Tristan. Can you maybe not get me killed by being your wonderful self?" He couldn't speak to his brother, not with his voice at any rate. So he used their link as brothers and spoke to him telepathically.

"Tell them I came here to talk to Master MacManus. I don't know why the alpha attacked me, but I have no problem with him. I just want a word with the vampire," she whispered through his mind.

Aiden swallowed slowly and glanced at the men close to him out of the corner of his eye. He couldn't give up the master. It went against everything in his nature to do so. He would rather die.

"You just might, vamp. I mean him no harm. I have something for him, something to give him. Tell me which one he is and I'll let you go. I've no beef with you."

"Fuck you," was his reply. When her teeth came down a little tighter, he couldn't stop the small cry of pain. His brother moved closer and she snarled without moving her mouth.

"Tell me what she wants, Aiden. I know you think that you shouldn't, but I'd just as soon you not die in my bar. Tell me what she said."

Her jaws loosened slightly and he could talk but still not move. He was angry, furious really. But as the master, Aiden had no choice but to do as Aaron had asked him. "She wants to talk to the master MacManus. She claims that she has something for him. I told her no, that I wouldn't do that." Looking at the panther at his neck, he said, *"You are fucking going to die for this. I'm going to hunt you down and tear you apart."*

"Then you will need to stand in line. There are many more ahead of you that would gladly tear me apart for reasons you'd never imagine in another six hundred years of lifetimes."

"I'm Master MacManus. If you let him go, I'll talk to you. No one needs to get hurt, I swear to you. I'm not sure what happened here, but I'm willing to do what you want to save the vamp you have in your jaws."

Aiden felt her loosen her teeth a little more. Before she fully moved off him, she whispered again. *"I've not hurt you. I took your blood to communicate with you, but you are unharmed. I'll move away, but don't make me have to kill you, vamp."*

Moving back, she remained a panther for a full minute just looking at him. When she shifted, it was immediate. No time seemed to pass from her being a black, sleek animal to a beautiful woman. Deadly, but very beautiful.

"I'm a bounty hunter. I have a vampire that is hurt and in need of blood. I can't help him and I was told to bring him to you. I can't bring him to you, but I can take you to him. If you would—"

"No!" Aiden shouted. Then in a calmer voice, he continued. "He's not going anywhere with you. I'll go and bring this supposed vamp back. Aaron, you can't go with her. She tried to kill me."

"He goes. He is the only one that I was told to trust. If he doesn't come, then the vamp dies. I don't care either way. What is it to be, master?"

Aiden started toward her again and Aaron put a hand on his arm to stop him. This was just wrong. The master didn't go on little day trips with shifters.

"I'll go. But these men have your scent, so if I don't come back, they will hunt you down. Have no doubt about that."

The woman stepped toward Aaron and reached out. Aaron, too, reached out his hand, probably thinking she was going to shake his hand. As soon as her hand wrapped around his, both she and Aaron disappeared.

~~~

Aaron didn't have time to be afraid. He didn't even have time to think of anything, and suddenly, they were in a cave. When she released his hand he staggered slightly.

"It'll pass in a second or two. The vamp needs blood, but I can't feed him. I don't know his name, but he's a part of or has something to do with the Council. I was sent to get him from his kidnappers. I've disposed of one of them, the other is not far. He isn't yet aware of the other's death or that I've found this man."

Aaron walked over to the vampire lying on the ground. He was alive, but barely. She was correct, he did need blood.

"His name is—"

"No. I don't want to know it. Just do what you have to do then I'll take you both wherever you want. I'm not going to be able to carry him far, but I'll get you both to safety."

Aaron turned slightly away from Samuel Macintosh, the until now missing heir of another realm, and looked at her. His magic was powerful and he could detect the scent of blood, warm and hot. Fresh. Closing his eyes, he moved over her and found that she was injured as well. Blood poured from a wound at her side; the bullet not silver was still in her body.

"I can see that you're shot. I could feed you as well. My blood is strong and it wouldn't harm me to feed the both of you."

"No thanks. I like to know that someone can't hunt me down, if it's all the same to you. If you would hurry it along, I need to be somewhere else tonight. I can...as far as I can get you is back to the bar. I thank you for helping him. My boss will contact you as soon as tomorrow to make arrangements to get him back."

Aaron nodded and then turned back to Samuel lying so still before him. Opening a vein on his wrist, he pressed it to his mouth and commanded him to drink. A few precious drops moved out of the injured vampire's mouth and down his cheek before he began drinking. Aaron contacted his mate to let her know what was going on.

"Love? I'm fine. I can feel your stress. I'm with a being. Can you tell me what she is?" As his mate, they were as close as two people would ever get.

"She? I can feel a male, but...no, I can feel her now. She's very strong. I can... I feel vampire, werewolf, and cat. I can also... Aaron, she just contacted me. She said that if you want to know what she is just turn around and ask her. She said that you were a rude ass and wondered why I was staying with you. I think I like this being."

Aaron could hear the humor in Sara's voice and he felt himself relax with it. Pulling his wrist from Samuel's mouth he sealed the ragged wound with his own tongue. He turned and stood in front of her.

"You've contacted my mate. She likes you, she said. So, bounty hunter, what are you? Sara detected vampire, werewolf, and werecat? I've seen your panther; what else can you take the shape of?"

"I don't believe they named my species. And the lab and its workers are no longer alive to go back and ask, not that I would. I'm a mixture of all predators. In addition to quite a bit of magic, my DNA has been altered to suit some need they thought they might like to work with. I can shape-shift into anything I need."

Aaron could see the blood on her hands where she had pressed it against the wound. He stepped toward her only to come up short when a gun was suddenly in her hand. He'd not even seen her pull it. Raising his hands to show that he was not going to harm her, he took a step back.

"You know you're just being stubborn, don't you? Let me help you. I swear to you that you will be safe with my blood."

"I'm hurt, not stupid. I'd appreciate it if you would just keep your blood where it belongs. If you're ready I'll take you both back now."

The movement of air was all the warning there was. One minute Aaron was standing to talk to the girl and the next he was being slammed hard against the opposite wall. Pain exploded in his head. Whatever had hit him had meant business. He started to rise when a sharp *"No!"* was issued in his mind.

"I can't fight if I have to babysit you. Sit still and don't move. He will not harm you if he has me to play with."

Aaron was sure he should have been insulted about her comment about babysitting him, but he could feel the air stir again and the other being was all he could get shimmered in the room once again. Aaron stayed where he was. He wasn't even sure he could have helped her much anyway. He had given blood without feeding and he had hit his head hard enough to make him see two of everything.

The man/beast was huge and could move faster than Aaron could see. The woman had no such problems, apparently, and attacked him every time it stopped. It had claws for hands; Aaron didn't think they were anything but his own hands and his teeth, razor sharp and dripping in saliva. They were at least two inches long. Its body, while short, was muscled and packed. The wings at its back were tucked tight, but Aaron could see that they would be huge when opened.

"You! I though you dead. Hoped it. I kill you now, mother fucker. My mate, he and I will eat your innards for our sup," the being hissed at the woman.

"Nope, not dead. Your mate is, however. He cried like a little babe when he died. You will do the same. It has been sanctioned and you know how much I love it when I have those kinds of orders."

37

Power burst from the being and looked to narrowly miss the girl. Suddenly, she was on the being's back with a wicked knife at his throat. Aaron hadn't seen it until that moment and wondered if she or the being had brought it. He'd not seen her have anything so assumed that she had taken it from the monster. She brought the blade across the monster's throat and removed its head. Black blood oozed from its neck and onto the ground as it dropped. Aaron watched as she reached above her head, seemingly to gather energy from around her. The blue ball, small at first in her hands, seemed to grow with the seconds. When it was perhaps three inches in diameter, she threw it into the blood and body and it exploded, destroying everything it touched.

The woman dropped to the ground and when he moved toward her, she simply raised her hand to still him. He waited. He could feel her weakening state and wondered how she was even able to sit upright. The scent of fresh blood tickled his throat.

"I would really like to go now please. I don't have...I must feed soon and go to ground. Please, give me a moment and I'll be ready."

"All right, we can go. I won't even ask you again to take some of my blood. I know you to be stubborn enough to refuse." He moved closer and kneeled down in front of her. "I didn't catch your name. I would like to tell whomever you work for what a great job you've done for our kind. And that you saved my life. For that, I thank you." Aaron touched her mind and was immediately seized with a sharp pain in his. Wincing slightly, he backed out of her head. Sara had been right, she was strong.

"Keep out, master, or it will only get worst. And I didn't throw it. I'm going to have to touch more of your skin this time. I need a better contact with you to move the three of us. I don't mean to be rude, but could you please open your shirt? I won't harm you."

Aaron started unbuttoning the shirt he had on. He knew instinctively that he could trust her. She had saved the vampire when she could have easily have let him die. She had also saved him. He wondered if this being was created like another of his Kiss, Bailey. He was going to look into it as soon as he got back.

When he moved toward the vamp on the ground she stopped him. "I've got him. Just stand still. I'm weak, master, if you will please just not try anything stupid, you'll be conscious when we get to our destination; otherwise, I'll have to knock you out. Deal?"

Aaron nodded then watched her lean down and pick Samuel up. So, she was strong of both mind and body. He was impressed. Moving toward her when she waved him close, she turned his back to her hip, wrapped her hand around him, and splayed her figures wide over his chest.

"We'll land where we departed. I know that there is no furniture there so we won't have to worry about you getting staked when we land. Hopefully." Before he could react to that scary statement, they were in the bar.

No one moved. Aaron was glad for that as he was dizzy again. He didn't know the mode of transportation she was using, but it was incredibly fast. When she let go of him he stepped away and staggered slightly. Aiden and Tristan jumped forward to catch him.

"I'm fine. Someone take the man and be careful, he's injured. As is she. Aiden, don't. I can see in your stance that you wish to harm her, but for all of our sakes, don't."

"She owes me. I haven't the slightest idea why she picked me to attack, but she owes me bl—"

"I attacked you because you were by far the most dangerous of all of you. You should all rethink your security. Had I been out for blood all of you would have been dead."

"Him? The most dangerous? How do you figure? I'm the alpha of one of the largest packs in the United States. Aaron here is the baddest vamp around and Tristan is old and has powers most never attain in several lifetimes. No offense, Aiden," Bradley said immediately.

"You also have guards. If I attacked you right now they would surround you. You, in turn, would trade your life for theirs, the same for the vamp here. He, on the other hand..." The woman pointed to Aiden. "He had no security and nothing to lose. He would have fought until his or my death without a single thought as to whether or not he lived. That is why I attacked, taking out the strongest. I must go. Master, I thank you again for your assistance."

Aaron bowed back to her as she disappeared.

The woman was right; he would have traded his life for those that surrounded him. His job as master first and foremost was to keep those around him safe. He just never realized that it would get him killed.

CHAPTER 6

Zane was weak the next morning, but better since she had fed lightly before going to her lair. She was careful not to lift too much and she didn't use any magic other than what was necessary to be alert to her surroundings. She was glad for the light work in the morning and even happier for the slow afternoon. When Duncan showed up about ten minutes before she was ready to go she was both happy and a little depressed about it.

"I have two books for you. I have had them for a very long time and would like to gift them to you. They are first editions. It is in thanks for letting me read your book collection."

Zane was touched. First of all, no one had ever "gifted" her anything before, and he'd given her something that he had treasured enough to keep for all this time. She had read both the books, but had already decided to keep them no matter what.

"Thank you, Duncan. I love them. I have some for you as well, though not as treasured. I picked these up a few days ago after we talked and you said you liked to read in French also."

Zane had found *A Christmas Carol* and *Pride and Prejudice* on the Internet. When she returned with them, she realized that he wasn't alone, that he had two children with him. A little boy and a little girl.

Zane didn't have any interaction with children. She'd spent most of her life training or alone. Children not only made her nervous, but they were the one thing that she was terrified of. When Duncan introduced them as Lizzy and Mac MacManus,

Zane sat down hard on the stool near her work area. She wasn't sure what she would have said to either of them, or to Duncan for that matter, when his cell phone rang. When he stepped away to answer she and the kids stared at one another.

"You smell like our Aunt Bailey. Are you like her? She's really pretty and nice and her baby is our cousin. Her name is Emma. We go over there and play with her all the time. You got kids?"

The little boy cocked his head at her when she didn't answer him right away. She wasn't sure what she could say to him, so she just stared. The little girl, Lizzy, tried to breach her mind, but Zane pushed back and Lizzy stopped. Smart girl. If she had tried again Zane would have hurt her. Zane didn't like people in her mind and could be quite vicious when they persisted. Duncan returned and told them that they had to go.

"My mistress is having car issues and will be calling Master Danny to have him come and retrieve it for her. She is in need of us to pick her up at the mall. Thank you for the—"

"Zane? I got a problem. Can you help me out before you go? I got a pick-up out on Route Forty and I have a break down at the mall. Can you go out to the mall and see if you can limp that one here for me? I'm going to be a good three hours with this pick-up and I don't want to leave Mrs. Mac's car in the lot. Hey there, Dunc. Didn't know you were here," Danny said as he came around the corner to the bay.

Zane could have said no, she was sure of it. She was even surer that she had planned to say it, but she found herself saying yes and packing up some tools in a big box to follow Duncan out to the mall. She liked Danny and she liked Duncan, she just wasn't so sure about Mrs. MacManus and wondered what she would think if she knew that Zane was the being her mate had met last night.

~~~

"Danny just called back. He said that someone is coming out to see if they can fix the car and then they'll drive it to the garage. But Duncan is coming here to get us now. I hate that this is happening tonight. I had hoped that Aaron and I would get to spend some time alone together."

Bailey smiled. From what she'd heard Aaron and Sara didn't care if they were alone or not. They were always going at it like rabbits. Well, so did she and Tristan, but that wasn't the point. Bailey stretched out her long legs and closed her eyes. Sara was talking to Aaron through their link and Bailey decided to touch Tristan.

"Sara and I are at the mall. Her car broke down and though both of us can fly home, she's decided to wait for Duncan. I miss you." Bailey sent her mate love and warmth.

"Ummm, that's a wonderful thing to wake up to, a warm woman sending me love. Why don't you come here with me now and leave Sara to her broken car? I can make it worth your while."

And she knew that he would too. When he started sending erotic images to her, she shifted on her seat. Damned man sure did have an imagination.

"Stop that! You ass, I'm in the car with your master's mate. What do you think she'll say when she can tell what's going on? Behave or so help me I'll sleep above floors for a week. What do you think that'll do to your plans?"

Bailey felt his growl as it echoed through her and just the sound of it moved through her body as though he'd touched her. Shifting again on her seat, she glanced over at Sara. The smile on her face told Bailey that Sara was having a similar conversation with Aaron. She nearly laughed out loud at the thought. Men and sex went hand in hand no matter what age, it seemed.

Ten minutes later, Duncan and the children pulled up beside them and a few minutes after that a battered pick-up with "March Towing and Service" written on the side. When the woman got out and slammed the door, Bailey was surprised and when she stepped toward them, Bailey moved toward her.

The two women stared at one another, both recognizing what the other was. They didn't know one another, but they did know that they were one in the same. Both were creations rather than human. When the woman reached out and touched Bailey's mind, she knew it for a certainty.

"I'm not going to harm them. I work for Danny March. I don't want any trouble. I just want to do my job and go."

Bailey glanced over at Sara and knew that she had detected something. *"Who are you? And are you a part of the lab at Co-Tech Industries? That's where I came from, but it's been gone for over twenty years now."*

"No. I don't know anything about Co-Tech Industries. I was made in some place that I'm not sure had a name. It was a lab, but only on the inside. It's gone now too. So are the monsters that worked there."

Bailey knew without a doubt that the "monsters" had been killed by this woman. When she was about to ask her name again Sara walked up to them. One look over her shoulder showed Duncan and the children going toward the entrance to the mall.

"Bailey? What's going on?" Sara turned to the woman and reached out her hand. "I'm Sara MacManus. I believe you know my mate, Aaron. I can smell him on you. Then there is the slight connection from our conversation last night as well. You saved his life. I'm indebted to you."

"I don't know what you're talking about. I'm here to fix your car and nothing more. I want nothing to do with either of you. And I'd very much like it if you would both forget whatever notions you have in your heads too. I'm a mechanic, nothing more. Mrs. MacManus, can you tell me what's going on with your vehicle? I'll see if I can get it running for you."

"All right. For now at least. It won't start. It makes a clicking noise when I turn the key, but doesn't engage it seems. I'm okay now to get home if you want to work on it. Bailey and I will ride home with Duncan."

The engine turned over and idled. No one was in the car and no one had turned the key. Bailey didn't say a word. She wasn't sure what she would have said either if Duncan and the children hadn't chosen that moment to return.

"If you wouldn't mind driving it to the garage, I'll follow you. It shouldn't give you any more problems as long as you don't turn it off between here and there. And then Mr. Duncan can give you a lift home. Is that all right with you?"

Bailey could tell that Sara was ready to burst with questions, but said nothing. It wasn't until they were seated in the now running car that Sara exploded with them. It might have been funny if Bailey didn't have questions of her own.

"I take it you two know one another? She's a lot stronger than Aaron or I felt last night, though I can still feel a bit of weakness to her. What can you tell me about her and where do you know her from?"

"I don't know her. Today was the first...you do realize that she's like me, right?" Bailey looked in the rearview mirror at the woman following them a good two car lengths back. "You said she saved Aaron last night? Then it's safe to assume that she is the one who saved Samuel too. I wonder who she works for. I'm going to contact Griff and see what he can find out about her."

"Aaron said she called herself a bounty hunter. That's basically the same thing you do, isn't it? You work for contracts, she collects bounties."

Bailey looked again. Something wasn't...she was missing something and she couldn't figure out what it was.

"Bailey are you listening to me?"

Bailey hadn't been. She'd been off in her own world. Then she it hit her. "She said she didn't come from Co-Tech Industries. She said that she didn't know anything about it. Sara, do you think there was more than one lab and that we missed it? I need to contact Griff and have him...have him look into it. Christ." Bailey sat back on the seat. Closing her eyes, she reached for her best friend and partner Griff. His answering with laughter made her smile.

"Hello, my dear. Has shopping gotten to you yet? I know how much you love that job. But think, it's for the little missus birthday and you do love her."

"Yes, I do love her. I miss you. You haven't been for a visit in weeks. Tristan was just saying you should come out and stay a few days."

Griff was her protector and her best friend. He was also a Celtic being called a Cynogriffon. They, her brother Tyler also, had escaped from Co-Tech Labs just before the three of them had been set to be terminated. Their DNA had failed to give the lab the results they'd been looking for so they were no longer useful. Setting fires and explosions throughout the building, Bailey and a bunch of others had escaped as the building blew. She and Griff had worked together since. He was the one who set up any jobs that she did. She used to work with her brother Tyler until his death nearly eleven years ago when Salvatore Madison had killed him in cold blood.

"Maybe. But you have called to me for information. I know what you seek. She is called the Mechanic. The file I got said her name was unknown, but she goes by Zane. You will need to speak to the being for any more than that. She is very...private. Do not take this one on, mistress. She is a danger even to herself." Bailey would wonder about the pause there later. But his words made her nervous.

"What do you mean 'a danger to even herself?'" That can't be good, Bailey thought. *"How do you know her and how long has she worked with you? She saved the master last night. Should everyone be on their best guard with her now in the picture?"*

"No. She will not harm those she is not hunting. Nor will she harm herself, though it is thought that she may someday. The queen came to me just after you met your mate and got Miss Emma." Bailey realized that it had been about four years now. *"She told me that this girl needed work. That she needed to be useful. The queen sends me what she needs taken care of and I send her out. The queen asked that I tell no one of her and her relationship with the queen. I told her that when you asked, I would tell you, but would keep the secret until such time. Zane's strength and powers are not like yours; hers are more, much more*

magically enhanced. I have my suspicions as to where the magic came from, but that is all."

Bailey thought about the car starting. She didn't know a lot about cars, but she thought that someone should have at least had to have turned the key. Glancing over to the ring of keys in the steering column, she noted yet again that the thing was in the off position. She was pretty sure it couldn't run like that.

"I know what you're thinking." Sara's comment startled Bailey. "You're thinking she started the car to get us away from her. She didn't want us asking questions—especially you. Why do you think?"

"Trust? Afraid? I don't know. If I were her, I'd not trust another one like me. But for some reason I do. Trust her, I mean. Griff said she works for the queen and that she goes by Zane. Her code name is Mechanic." Bailey watched as Sara pulled the car into the garage lot and took off her seatbelt. "Sara, she can't know that we know. Griff said she is stronger than me magically. And that she is powerful."

Sara nodded. There wasn't much else they could do for now. Zane wasn't a threat to them and she had saved the master and another of his kind. Until she did something to do away with his trust, Aaron would protect her as though she was one of his Kiss.

CHAPTER 7

Aiden woke to a strange room. It took him several seconds to remember that he'd stayed at the MacManus mansion to sleep through the day. They had all been talking until very late and though Aiden could simply take himself home, he'd decided to stay and talk with Aaron when he rose.

Turning on the shower, he looked at himself in the mirror. The marks from the woman's fangs were all but gone. The area where she had hit him to knock him down was tender; his chest muscles burned slightly when he moved. But he was otherwise fine. Maybe a little embarrassed that he'd been downed so easily, but being told that he was considered the most dangerous of the group of them standing there made that not sting quite so much.

Stepping under the hot spray he thought about her again. Not as a cat this time, but as the beautiful woman. Her inky hair and eyes were as dark as a stormy summer night. Her body, while tight and muscled, was still very feminine and soft. When she had shifted into the animal and then back again he could see her shape and found her to be very... He needed to stop this train of thought before he got himself into trouble. He was here to talk to Aaron about setting up a base, a home away from his parents where he could search far and wide for his mate.

Scrubbing his body slightly harder than necessary, he got out of the shower a little sorer than when he'd gone in and a lot angrier with the woman. He wasn't sure why he was mad at her, but he was all the same.

Getting dressed, Aiden moved to the upper levels of the house and nearly turned around and hid in the lair he'd just left. The voices, heated in anger, were coming from the kitchen and Sara and Aaron were not sounding too pleased with someone else in the room. Entering with caution, Aiden stood back and waited.

"She said that she won't tell us, not that she didn't know. Damn it, Sara, I demand that you bring her here right this minute and make her tell me. This is important and I have a right to know."

"Now Aaron, you know Mel when she gets a—"

"I swear to Christ, James, if you give me that story about her temper once more, I may brain you. Mel and her temper be damned. I have a hunter in my realm, one who is hunting without my permission. I want to know why and who sanctioned this."

Aiden hadn't been in the States long, and he'd not spent a great deal of time with the master, but he was pretty sure the man seldom lost his temper. He wondered how much better this was going to get when Aaron suddenly turned on him.

It was all he could do not to burst out laughing. Aiden wondered if Aaron knew he had a pink necklace around his neck. A quick glance around the room showed that there were several more in varying bright colors all over the table.

"You! You go and get this woman and bring her to me. I want her here yesterday. I'm going to get answers even if I have to get them from her myself."

Aiden looked over at Sara. He didn't have any clue who he was to go and get and where he was suppose to find her when he did. Sara looked ready to say something when the phone on the wall rang. Duncan seemed to materialize in the room and answered it.

"It is for you, my lady. It seems that the SBV is finished and we may pick it up at our earliest convenience. Master Danny said that it was a bad solenoid. I'm not sure what that is, but he said that it is running smoothly now. Shall I make arrangements to pick it up tonight?"

"*No!* Aiden will go. He'll bring her back too. I mean it. If she doesn't come back with you, I want you to bash her over the head with a heavy object and bring her back anyway. I'm in no mood to put up with this."

"Aaron, be reasonable. Aiden can't hit her. Besides, she'd probably hit him back. I'll go and if she doesn't come back with me, we'll try your plan next. We'll call it Plan B, all right?"

"Sara, I don't appreciate you making fun of me. I've had a rough two days and I'm not in the...shit!" When Aaron backed to the counter, Aiden felt the first tickle of magic enter the room.

The woman powered in the room so quickly that it was like a blink of an eye. When she threw Sara to the ground, tugging Duncan down with her and covering her with her body, Aiden did the same to Aaron. He wasn't sure what was happening, but knew without a doubt that it was danger.

A spray of bullets filled the kitchen walls with holes almost immediately. Broken glass and pottery flew in every direction. Several heavier items hit Aiden in the back, but he never moved off Aaron. He could see that the woman didn't move either. What only took a few seconds seemed to go on for hours.

When the room was quiet with nothing more than a few pieces of glass falling to the floor the woman moved slightly. Aiden started to move off of Aaron when he felt a tear in his ribs; pain radiated from the area. Looking down, he could see that he'd been shot and if the weakening of his body was any indication, he'd been hit with silver.

Silver was poison to most supernaturals. It would kill them quickly if in a major organ or slowly if left in the body. Before Aiden could voice that he'd been hit he was lying on his back on the floor and the woman was pressing her hand to his ribs.

"I'm going to remove the bullet. You have to lay still. I'm not...we've both been hit, but silver doesn't harm me like it will you. I have to have your permission and a trade. I need for you to give me something and accept what I'm about to do for you. Do you understand?"

Aiden was starting to feel the silver poison his body. "Yes. I...your name. Can you tell me your name?"

"Allison Zander. Everyone calls me Zane. Do you have a trade? You need to think it up quickly. I can't help you without it."

"I don't have anything of...I don't know what you need or want. Tell me...give me a choice, please?"

Aiden was fading quickly, so he nearly missed the whisper through his mind. *"You can ask her for a boon. A favor, one to use for later that she cannot refuse."*

"You'll owe me one, Zane. I'll collect in the future—if I have a future. Please, save me." Then everything blacked out.

~~~

Closing her eyes, Zane poured her energy into the wound. The first thing she did was stop the bleeding. It would do her no good to save him from the bullet if he bled to death on the floor.

Zane could hear the others talking, but paid little attention to them. She needed to focus all of her energies on him, what she was doing and on the area surrounding the house and its occupants.

The bullet had lodged between his ribs and she had to break one to get the silver bullet out. Not moving her hands from his bloodied side, the bullet suddenly popped out of the hole it had entered and dropped to the floor. Throwing back her head, Zane gathered energy from the air and a little from Aaron to pour back into the blood of Aiden. Chasing down the poisoned blood proved to be tricky, but it wasn't long before she could feel that it was all gone. Slowly backing out of his body and back into hers, she began the process of mending the rib and closing the wound. She couldn't give him blood, but she knew that when he was able to feed next, he'd be as good as new.

Moving away from the vamp on the floor she just managed to back to the counter behind her before she felt the first wave of weakness move over her. "He'll need to feed when he wakes. The poison is gone. I don't think he'll have any problems once he feeds." Zane started to rise, but thought she'd just sit a moment longer. Moving her hand to her thigh she could feel the bullet moving its way out of her muscle. Soon it would be gone as well.

"What happened here, Zane? Who did...you knew it was going to happen. You came here to save us. Who was it?" Aaron asked as he pulled a linen towel down from above them and pressed it to her wound.

Zane could feel the anger boil off the master and wanted to smile. He was furious and yet his voice sounded like he'd just ask her what time it was. This man had a great deal of control and Zane was impressed.

"The same people who had that man kidnapped from the other night. I don't know how they knew you had anything to do with it, but apparently somewhere there is a leak. My boss is going to know what I know, which isn't much. I have a blood connection to him." She pointed to the man on the floor she'd just saved. "And I felt them coming toward him. When I got here, I realized that Mrs. MacManus had to be my first priority. I'm sorry about your kitchen. I hope you have good insurance."

Aaron looked around the kitchen as though he'd never seen it before. It was a mess. What hadn't been destroyed by gunfire had been destroyed by falling debris. Duncan was already sweeping things up and muttering about the roast he had in the oven and how it would never do now.

"You know, fuck the kitchen. Tell me what is going to happen n—wait, what did you mean that Sara had to be a priority? Whoever did this was out for her? I'll kill the son-of-a-bitch!"

"No, nothing like that. They were only after you and I guess whoever happened to be next to you. No, Mrs. MacManus is pregnant. As soon as I...are you all right?"

Aaron was looking at her strangely. She didn't know what she'd said to make him look like he'd just won the lottery, but she supposed it was better than the anger he'd had earlier. When he suddenly got up and pulled Mrs. MacManus into his arms she guessed it was the baby. Soon after, they left the room. Zane looked up at Duncan when he handed her a glass of blood.

"Thank you very much, Mr. Duncan." She drained it in one gulp. "I don't suppose you have some juice, do you? I can drink that in a pinch if you have it."

Duncan looked at her oddly then asked, "What sort of container is a pinch, Miss Zane? I believe we have all kinds of glasses and cups, but I do not believe I have run across a 'pinch.'"

Zane grinned. "Just a regular glass then. That'll be fine. Then I'll take him...what's him name anyway?"

"Master Aiden St. James. He is brother to Master Tristan and brother-in-law to Mistress Bailey. I believe he is staying here. I can lend you a hand if you so desire. I cannot lift him, but I can lead the way to his lair."

When Duncan handed her the full glass of orange juice she drank it straight down. It really wouldn't help her much; she would have had to drink the entire gallon for it to even make a dent in what she needed. But she stood anyway. Reaching down to pull Aiden over her shoulder, she staggered slightly and had to hold onto the wall several times on their trip to the lower levels. When Duncan managed to get the door open with her help, Zane wasn't sure how much longer she would be able to go without rest and blood. When she put Aiden onto his bed she held onto the post of it while she watched Duncan fuss with the man and the blankets.

"Miss, if you do not mind me saying so, you look as if you might be all done in. You could stay here tonight. There are plenty of beds and if you require a sub room, that could be arranged as well. This family is greatly indebted to you."

Zane looked at the bed. It looked soft and inviting. She didn't much care for the man there, but the thought of resting even if only for an hour or two, would be well worth being next to him.

"If you could just let me rest for an hour, I'll sleep here. He is out and won't notice me. I'm very tired and weak, but I'll be out before he rises, I promise."

"I doubt Master Aiden will mind. You did manage to save his life as well. When you are ready to leave I will make sure that you have an ample breakfast to send you on your way with. Have a good rest, Miss Zane."

As soon as the door closed behind him Zane started having second thoughts. She had never shared a bed with anyone before and was slightly nervous now about sharing one with the huge vamp. She looked down at him in his slumber.

Aiden was very beautiful. Zane supposed that wasn't the correct word for a man, but it suited him. His dark hair, loose now from his tie at the back, hung down in a cascade of dark silk. The color reminded her of dark, rich coffee she had seen at a few of the coffee shops she'd been by. His eyes, closed now in sleep, were a deep blue with silver around the edges. She knew that when he was pissed, which was what he was around her most of the time, they would darken to the deepest red. His face was a classical one. High cheekbones, long strong jaw. His nose looked like it might have been broken at one time; there was a small bump right in the middle that gave him a devil-may-care look. Long lashes, as dark as his hair, fanned over his cheeks.

When she felt herself reaching for his shirt to open, just to see if he was as solid as he looked, Zane staggered to the bathroom. She wanted to be gone before he woke and if she stood around gawking at him like a lovesick kid she'd still be here when he did. Turning on the shower tabs and realizing that the shower must have been used recently, she flushed when she realized that it had been him.

Her own wound was still bleeding, though not nearly as bad. She cleaned it as best she could and after wrapping a towel around her body, went into the bedroom, closing the door to the bathroom behind her. The room was black as pitch, but her eyesight was as good as any vampire's and she moved to the bed without once popping her toe against anything. Taking the towel off and tossing it toward the chair, she pulled the blanket up and over her nude body. Exhaustion hit her hard and before she knew it, Zane was sound asleep.

Kathi S. Barton

CHAPTER 8

Aiden pulled the warmth closer to him. He thought he'd never had a softer blanket than the one he had right now. And it smelled delicious, like his mother's flower garden in the last summer nights. When he moved his hand down he froze. Opening one eye he looked at his "blanket."

It was Zane. Zane was in his bed and wrapped around him like a comforter and...Christ! She was naked. Moving his hand a little more, he realized that her breast filled his hand. Filled it fully and the hardened nipple was just between his fingers. Before he could stop himself, he gently rolled the hard peak between his thumb and finger and nearly groaned out loud when she arched against him.

Still rolling her nipple in his fingers, he shifted his body so that she was now facing him. He wanted to take her nipple into his mouth and sample the wonderful treat, but he also wanted to explore her more before she woke. He grinned a half grin, knowing full well that if she were to wake now she'd more than likely put the bullet back into his body and leave it there. When he pinched it a little harder she moaned in her sleep.

Aiden was rock hard. His cock needed relief from his pants and needed to be buried deep in the woman in his arms. Closing his eyes, and without taking his hands off Zane, he willed his shirt and shoes off. He thought about his pants too, but knew that he was pushing his state of undress as it was. Besides, if he were honest with himself, he was actually afraid of Zane. She was a formidable woman.

Reluctantly removing his hand from her luscious breast Aiden smoothed his hands down her body. Her skin was warm, almost hot. He loved the softness of it, the way his hand felt moving along her skin.

That's when he noticed the tats on her body. There were several weapons on her, all lethal-looking with a great deal of artwork and a tremendous amount of detail.

Along her entire right side from the breast bone to her hip was a long knife. Even in the darkened room, he could see that it was silver. The handle was curved and bejeweled-looking. He wondered what had possessed her to have such a tattoo put on her body. Aiden wondered if this was like the knife Aaron had described when he'd told them about the cave.

That was when he noticed the one on her hip about two inches below her hipbone. It was of a Glock, one of the smaller ones. Running his hand over her skin and the tat he was amazed at how hot it was, and how detailed. Moving his face toward her neck and the warm flesh there Aiden did moan this time. It was deep and hungry-sounding even to his ears. He knew the exact moment Zane woke up and felt him there.

"If you bite me, you'll die. If you don't remove yourself from my body, you'll die. If you linger too long, you'll die."

Not much in the way of payoffs, just bad news he thought, and snuggled deeper into her neck and licked the pulse beating there. Her flavor, the taste of her, nearly had him throw her on to her back so he could take her. He raised his head and looked down at her.

"You're in my bed, naked. You can't expect a man not to take advantage of that, can you? You are luscious, has anyone ever told you that?"

"No, they've never seen me nude before. Get off me, you big lug. I have to get up. I need to get out of here and find who shot up the master's home."

Zane was a virgin. He didn't know why that both thrilled and terrified him, but it did. He leaned down to her mouth and brushed his over hers. Her hot breath fanned over his face and he couldn't think beyond the need to taste her.

"Zane, let me kiss you. Give me your mouth, give it to me, please?" Her sigh nearly undid him. When she shifted he moved closer still. Then he stopped.

"I will shoot you. This gun is loaded with silver and a silver liquid is inside each bullet. Let me up right now or I pull the trigger. I did ask you nicely, now I do it my way."

Aiden moved back but didn't let go of her. He recognized the gun. He glanced to her hip and saw that the one there, the tattoo, was missing. All that was left was the empty holster. Aiden looked into her eyes before he spoke. "You can pull that free of you as a weapon. You are never unarmed, are you? Are the others, the other tattoos, the same?"

"Yes. I have a blade at my side and one on my back. There are stars along the back of my hairline that are razor sharp. There are ten of them stacked with ten stars each. Behind each ear is a magazine for this gun and the one on the other size. They are stacked ten each as well. My ankles are wrapped in silver chain. Now that you've an inventory of my weaponry, I'd like for you to let me go. I have to go to work."

Aiden moved back more, bringing her with him, the gun included. When she sat up over his waist he put his hands on her hips and held her still. He didn't even look at the gun and ignored the fact that it was pointed at his chest. All he could hope for was that as his mate, she wouldn't be able to harm him.

"I want to bury myself deep inside of you, Zane. But I can wait for you. You are my mate, mine for all time. I'm sure that you know that I tell you the truth. I can't help but protect you, keep you safe. I also know that with you, it will be different. You are as much a predator as I. But I need to know that you are safe."

Zane shifted slightly over him and he couldn't stop the groan of need that rippled through him. Her wet heat now centered over his cock and though he was still clothed, he could still feel her. Looking down were she covered him he could see her tight curls glistening with her juices. He couldn't help himself, and before he knew it his fingers were tracing the line of curls that covered her.

"Stop... please, don't touch... please stop this, Aiden. I don't want this and you...ohyesohyesohyes!"

Aiden flicked his finger deep, touching her tiny nub over and over. Her gun went to her hip and disappeared back into her holster, he assumed. When Zane leaned forward her hands splayed over his chest, he pressed his thumb and finger deep into her soft lips and opened her to him. He leaned up and held her to his body even as he tormented her clit. She started to ride his cock, soaking it with her copious amount of cream.

"Zane, love, let me taste you. Let me sip from your vein and taste you. And when I do, I want you to come. I want the spicy taste of your climax in my mouth as it heats your blood."

Aiden buried his face in her shoulder. Licking the pounding pulse he waited for her to let him drink from her. When she cocked her head away from him, giving him her throat, he didn't wait to see if she changed her mind, but licked the spot again and sank his fangs deep inside of her.

~~~

The world splintered when he bit her. Colors swirled around her closed eyes and a roaring echoed through her head. Zane wrapped her fingers in his hair and pulled him closer. She needed him anchored to her tight as he fed from her. It wasn't enough to have him drinking, she needed him. Needed him deep, deep within her. Not knowing how to tell him what she wanted, what she needed, Zane sent him her need.

Suddenly, she was on her back. Aiden looked down at her and it was all she could do not to drag him down on top of her again. She knew that he was as naked as her, the hair on his legs rubbing erotic dances on her thighs. He seemed to be waiting, waiting for her to say what she wanted, what she needed.

"Tell me, Zane. Tell me what you want from me. I want no misunderstanding between us, not now, not ever. If I take you, I take all of you. You'll be bound to me for all eternity. Is that what you want? Tell me now."

Is it what she wanted? She wasn't sure all of the sudden. She hadn't needed people, not in all her life. She was a loner and she knew that living with him, she'd never have any time of her own again.

"Can't we just have sex? Why does it have to be all or nothing? What if I don't like you? What if I can't...I'm not a nice person. I've done things, lots of things that I can't...I want you, but not like that, not forever. I can't do forever."

Aiden rolled off her so quickly that she cried out in alarm. When she looked to where he was standing she noticed he was dressed completely, head to toe. When he pulled his hair back, she watched as he took several deep breaths before he turned to face her.

"I have to leave. I don't... I will be able to find you if you need me, but I can't be near you. Not if this is all you want. I want you as my mate, not as my sometime lover. Call out to me if you change your mind. Good night, Zane."

When the door closed quietly behind him she sat there for several minutes not thinking about a thing. Nothing, not a thought, nothing entered her mind. When she heard someone stirring in the hall beyond her she closed her eyes and took herself to her own lair. Moving to the sublevels of the house she'd bought and converted, she moved as though she was on automatic pilot. It wasn't until she was settled into her own dark corner that she thought about Aiden and what she had done to him. His rejection and his hurt with her were like her own. She could feel it run through her heart and head.

When her pager went off, she nearly didn't get up to answer it. Finally moving to the phone, the only one in the house, she dialed the number. The voice at the other end was female and she knew it as well as the male who normally called to give her the assignments.

"My lady. How may I be of service this evening?" She hated this woman, the Queen of Magic. Zane wanted to hang up, to scream at her, to tell her that it was unfair, but she did nothing but wait.

61

"You can cut the subservient act, Zane. We both know you have no respect for me. I have an assignment, but first I'd like to know if your wound is healed from today. I was told you were shot."

Thrown slightly off her guard Zane didn't at first answer. She wondered for all of two seconds how she had found out, but wondered why she even cared. Zane had been hurt before and had not been asked if she was healed.

"The assignment, if you please. Unless it's part of my sentence too, to make sure that you are informed of my wellbeing. Is it, my lady?" There was no mistaking the snarl this time and Zane hoped that the queen would get the message.

"It's always my duty to make sure that my subjects are in goo—"

"Make no mistake, Queen, I'm no subject of yours. I am your slave only. And I will remain so until such a time that I've served my sentence or I'm dead. Now, if you would be so kind as to tell me what mess you'd like for me to mop up for you I can get started."

There was silence at the other end. Zane could feel the tears on her cheeks and refused to wipe them away. She'd thought that she'd cried them all out, but apparently not. Looking at the wall across from her she could see the two dates. The date her sentence began and when it would be at an end. Just two thousand nine hundred and forty-six more years to go of her three thousand year life sentence, a piece of cake.

"Zane, it doesn't have to be this way. I swear to you if you would just tell me what happened I can—"

"The assignment or I hang up and you can have your other flunky call me. In fact, I would prefer if he did from now on. I believe you calling me would be considered cruel and unusually punishment—even for me."

The line went dead. Zane laid the phone in the cradle and stood waiting. She knew that it would ring again soon. The man, whoever he was, would call her with a location and she would go. She had no choice. This is why she could never mate. This is why she would never be with anyone for more time than it took for them to find out what she'd done. When the phone rang it was the man again. He sounded...well, amused came to mind and Zane wondered about it. Before she could inquire about it he gave her the next assignment.

"I have a vampire that needs to be taken down. He has killed a number of humans and the Council wants him destroyed tonight. How quickly can you get to D.C.?"

Kathi S. Barton

CHAPTER 9

Zane had been just seventeen when her world had turned upside down. She'd never been outside the lab, not that she'd know what to do when she got there. Zane had been looking into the minds of the lab assistants for years trying to discover where they went, what they did. None of it seemed all that great. Not that in her cell was any different, but it was all she'd ever known.

The man in charge, Timothy Daniels, was coming down the hall again and he wasn't alone. He had his usual protégé of four—Scott, Homer, John, and Phillip. She hated him, Timmy, and what he did to them. She thought that he enjoyed the torture much more than anyone did and they all got some rush out of besting them. Zane heard them call the person next to her to the back of his cell and wait.

"When I open this door you'll do as you're told or I will make you suffer. You know how much I hate to do this to you. Are you going to cooperate, Zulu Alpha Eight?"

None of the occupants had names. They all went by the numbers just above their doors. Zane had gotten her name from them, Zulu Alpha Nine—Zane. But the humans kept mispronouncing it and had said Zander, so she left it at that.

"Please, I'm injured. I want to just rest for another day. I haven't been fed today or yesterday. Just one more day."

Zane had gone to the wall that connected to Eight and pressed against it. She fed him through the connection they all had that they didn't think the lab boys knew about. She could feel him gaining from it and when she'd given him enough she stepped back and huddled into the corner on the opposite wall. Just as she sat down and drew the shadows around herself someone banged on her door.

"Zulu Alpha Nine, you come out where I can see you now. Don't make me have to come in there and get you again. I won't be as easy this time." She knew that voice. Scott.

"Come in and try. I'm not bleeding this time and I'll feed on your hot blood. I could always use a nice snack before I kill you."

Energy poured into her. Every inmate in the place hated what they were and wanted out. Zane knew that if Scott came in he'd be armed. Well, so was she. She'd found the magic book and had hidden it in her room several weeks ago. She was ready for him and all the others. The tattoos were done and she had enhanced them with the help of the witch across the hall. Now all she had to do was wait.

Zane heard the keys in the lock and smiled. Not a good smile that reached her eyes, but one of anticipation, one of hunger. When Scott stepped into the room with his weapon drawn Zane didn't move. She'd wait for him to come closer. As he swept the room with his flashlight she shifted. Moving behind him she shifted into herself again and pulled the blade out from behind her.

Just before she touched him she leaned in and whispered in his ear. "You should have stayed outside, Scott. I told you what I'd do."

Snapping his head back, she sank her teeth deep into his jugular as he started to scream. His blood, tainted with coke and other drugs, hit her system hard. None of it would hurt her or affect her, but it did leave a bitter taste in her mouth.

Zane couldn't drain him. It was a myth that a vampire could drain a human. There was simply too much blood in a body and it would take a very long time to do it, even with several people. But she could kill him. Pulling away and not sealing the deep, jagged wound, she dropped him to the floor when she'd had her fill, not caring that he was bleeding to death.

Picking up his Taser and his gun, Zane put them next to her body and shifted again. This time into her panther, and since she had fed well, she was as powerful as she could ever be. As she slid into the hall Zane moved up behind the man closest to her. His scent marked him as prey; fear and terror were sharp around him. As she leapt to John, one of the many lab idiots, he pulled Eight in front of him and Zane couldn't stop her forward movement, but she could sheath her claws. As soon as both men were down, Zane raked her paw at Eight and pushed him away from her. When she could reach the neck of John, she bit down hard on his throat and tore it away.

With blood still dripping from her muzzle, she started to track the other two with James. Homer, the youngest of them, had wet himself. The odor burned her nose and made her sneeze. Circling around to the right, Zane growled low and deep in her throat. She was trying to get Homer to run. One less to help them the better, not that she thought he'd be much help.

"You'll back off, Nine, I'll kill you if you don't. I thought we were getting along so well for the past two weeks. Now, be a good girl and go into your cell and we'll forget this ever happened." Phillip was trying to herd her and she lunged at him twice before he moved back with the others.

"Just fucking kill her. That's what you're supposed to do when they go bad. Kill her and get this over with."

Timmy could be very brave when he had the other two shielding him, she thought.

When Phillip drew his gun, Zane leapt through the air at him. Her jaws clamped around his wrist and with a hard bite, she took his hand off with the gun still in his fingers. Blood spurted everywhere as she spit the appendage and gun out of her mouth. Pain hit her hard in the hip. Then again in the ribs. Tim had pulled his gun out and had fired at her.

The scent of blood was causing a frenzy with the others on her floor. The noise was loud and she wanted to scream at them to shut up. But she needed to stay a cat or he'd likely kill her human form. Crouching lower to the floor, she snarled at them. Tim grabbed

Homer around the throat and pulled him in front of him as a cover. Out of the corner of her eye Zane could see Six reaching out from his small slot, his hand signing to her to force them his way. Sliding her body along the floor, keeping a close eye on the gun, Zane circled them around toward Six.

Six couldn't do much but to grab his leg, but it was enough to distract him. When he squealed and turned to see what had touched him Zane jumped. The bullet entered her chest just as she connected with the two men. Pain ricocheted though her, but she didn't have time to deal with it so she pushed it back. Swiping her sharp claw at Homer she removed his head from his body. Now all that was left to deal with before they could escape was Tim.

Blood poured from her wounds and she could feel herself getting weaker by the second. But if she gave up now all of them would die. Zane shifted and stood before her tormentor.

"You aren't going to get away with murdering these men, Nine. I'm going to make sure they know that you had to be put down because you killed all of them and all of the occupants of this floor. You aren't fit to live."

Zane simply moved to her right and watched as he moved with her. "I'm not going to let you go to tell anyone what happened here today. You are going to be just as dead as them." She waved a dispassionate hand toward the three dead men in the hall with them.

Tim glanced at the man closest to him and shuddered. Blood poured from his neck and the puddle beneath him was growing. The putrid smell of shit permeated the air around him.

"Maybe we could work out a deal. I have lots of money. When you leave here you'll need some. I'll give you plenty. You'd like that, wouldn't you? Lots of money to buy pretty things with?"

"No. I want you dead. That will be pretty enough for me." Reaching behind her she pulled out the sword and watched as Tim's eyes widened. "I learned the art of Living Art. It was easy enough with the book you stole. I have enjoyed reading it and learning it."

Tim paled as she walked toward him. She didn't have any compulsion about killing him. She was just sorry it had to be quick. As it was now she could hear the elevators coming down. Soon there would be too many for her to handle alone. She needed to get the other cells open now.

When Tim pointed the gun at her again she watched him. Moving through his mind, she seized it tight. As the gun turned to his own head with a trembling hand he began to sob and beg her. Even as the gun rested at his temple he continued to tell her what he would give her if she would let him live. When his brain exploded on the opposite wall Zane reached into his pocket and retrieved the key card. Taking the smaller blade from her ankle, it peeling away from her skin in seconds, Zane removed his right hand. Walking to each of the cell doors she swiped his card across the key reader, keyed in his code, and put his severed hand over the reader. Soon everyone was free.

Mayhem ensued after that. Each of the other thirteen beings on the floor annihilated the bodies until Zane took control. They would kill one another if they didn't remain calm.

When the elevator opened everyone was killed instantly. Zane tried to control their blood lust, but it was soon becoming apparent that she couldn't. Letting them go was her only option. She was too weak to fight them.

Everyone in the building that had worked there was dead or dying by the time the queen and her guard showed up. All but a few of the occupants had already escaped. Zane was feeding again, this time from a bag, when she first felt the power, not knowing nor understanding where it came from. When the queen walked into the main lobby Zane was waiting for her.

"Who are you and what happened here? What is going on? I demand to know why I didn't know about this place."

"I'm Zulu Alpha Nine, and I haven't the slightest clue why you weren't informed. Frankly, I don't give a shit either. I just... I used to live here."

"What sort of name is that? I can feel your weakness and your powerbase. You are extremely strong and you have a lot of magic, both dark and white. Who is in charge here? I demand that you tell me who they are."

Zane thought she looked regal and queenlike and didn't know at the time how true that assessment was. She could also feel her anger and her power. Zane didn't need someone else ordering her around and resented the woman immediately.

"And just who do you think you are to demand anything? I gave you my name, now who the hell are you? And what are *you* doing here?"

"I'm your queen, Melody, Mistress of Light, Keeper of Magic. And you will keep a civil tongue in your head. I felt the magic, a great deal of magic, being destroyed or used. Is this how you use a gift from me, to destroy humans? The penalty for such abuse is death."

Zane looked around the room. No one here or throughout the building had gotten any more than they had deserved. Even the cleaning crew had been horrible to them all, hitting them with their brooms or mops. Some had even sprayed them with their chemicals, blinding some and just burning others. But to have the others hunted down and killed, that seemed to her to be worse than what had been done to them. Zane felt that justice had been served here.

"You aren't my queen and they're all dead. I take full responsibly for what happened. The others...they didn't know what I was going to do when I did this."

The scent of death hung heavy in the air. The queen looked around her at the carnage and then back at Zane. There were two dead bodies within two feet of them and several more in different stages of ripped apart just a few more feet away. The once pristine carpet was covered in blood and gore. All of the bodies that Zane had found were in similar or worse condition. Most of them had been ripped to shreds. Body parts strewn all over the place. The entire place looked like a blood bath. She did not look like she believed Zane. Her next words confirmed it.

"You expect me to believe that you're responsible for this...this mess? You alone killed all of these humans? Magic

70

cannot be used to kill others. You should have learned that the first time you used it. Tell me why these people were killed and why you lied to me and I'll go easy on your punishment."

In actuality Zane didn't have a clue what had happened. She knew that the inmates had let everyone out of their cages and that people, all the humans, had been killed, but as to who did what, she didn't know. Soon after she took out Timothy, or had him do it, she blacked out from blood loss and the gunshot wounds. She was just as in the dark as the queen, but she wouldn't tell her that.

"You've already given me my trial and my sentences, haven't you? Are you always so quick to judge?" Zane could feel the others as they ran and hid. She would not give anyone up to this woman no matter what she had to suffer. "I did this. All of it. I ran the facility and I killed the humans. I'm the only one here. And for the record, if you don't kill me, then I will."

CHAPTER 10

"Uncle Aiden, what's the matter? Are you mad at me? I'm sorry if I made you mad, please smile for me."

Aiden looked down at his niece. Emma had been playing at his feet when he'd drifted off into thinking about Zane.

"No, sweetcakes, I'm not mad at you. I just have something on my mind. I'm the one who should be sorry for neglecting you for so long."

Aiden pulled her up onto his lap and ran his hand through her thick blond curls. She was so beautiful, this little girl. Her parents had been killed when she was a baby. They had been staked to the ground to meet the sunlight. Emma had been left in her car seat in the sun as well. Whoever had killed her parents must have assumed that she would die the way her parents had, boiling from the inside out and exploding when their insides got too hot.

But Emma hadn't reached her maturity yet. Even though she was a pure blood, she wouldn't actually become a vampire until she reached twenty-five. She would have had training on how to keep herself alive and how to hide and care for herself if she ever found herself in a situation where she couldn't get to shelter. Tristan and Bailey had adopted Emma when she'd first come to Becca's House, a home for abused and neglected children.

"Will you marry me, Uncle Aiden? I love you already and I don't mind when you kiss me. You have a nice smile too, but not when you look all scrunched up like this." Emma screwed up her face in a way that had Aiden burst out laughing.

"My, I should work on my scrunched up face, huh? Why I bet that face would scare off your grandma if she saw it. Wouldn't it, Mommy?"

"If only," was Bailey's low comment. But Aiden heard and so apparently had Tristan. He walked over to the two of them on the large sofa and scooped his daughter up into his arm.

"Your mommy needs her bottom paddled. Tell your Uncle Aiden goodnight, sweetheart, and I'll be up later and check on you." Aiden watched as his brother kissed his daughter and Bailey took her away. Sitting down on the couch next to him Aiden waited for it to begin. He didn't have long to wait. "You want to tell me what has you in such a funk?"

"Not particularly. I've got a lot on my mind is all and I'd appreciate it if you mind your own business. You can't help me with it anyway."

"Is it your mate? I can smell that woman on you. I know you have no choice in who she turns out to be, and it doesn't help to fight it. I know. But in the end it all works out. I love Bailey with my life and am gladder daily that she came into it. Whatever you think she's done isn't—"

"She refused me, not me her. She just wants to have sex and not long term. I wait six hundred years for someone to share my life with and she just wants it to be casual. How fucked up is that?" Aiden got up to pace. He really hadn't meant to tell Tristan anything, but now that the door was open he didn't want to stop. Besides, Aiden was pretty sure that he had gone too far in the bonding process to feed from anyone else.

As a mated couple they could no longer feed from anyone else. Zane would either be his mate in all ways, or he'd have to hunt her down every time he wanted to feed. It wasn't anything he wanted to have to do.

"What did she say? I mean, maybe she's just frightened about the whole bonding/mating thing and she will come around when she understands. I know it can be a lot of changes for someone that isn't already a vampire." Aiden looked at his brother as he spoke.

"She knows. She is part vamp. Zane made it perfectly clear that all she wants from me is sex. Oh yeah, and she's a virgin. Nearly killed me to walk away from her too. I told her that I'd taken her blood and if she wanted me or needed me, I would be there. But I wanted it all, not a sex partner whenever she gets the itch."

"Well gee, with a wonderful line like that it's small wonder she didn't stake you," Bailey said as she reentered the room. "You St. James boys sure have a lot to learn about women. I don't suppose you asked her *why* she didn't want to bond with you, did you? I mean, I know what she is and what she came from. You think maybe she *might* have a good reason to not want to be with you?"

Aiden felt his face heat. No. Not only had he not asked her, but when she had told him she wasn't a nice person he didn't even ask her what she meant. Then he'd walked away from her without letting her explain anything.

"I don't want to discuss this with you guys. I told her what I wanted and the rest is up to her. She should know that as my mate I would forgive her anything—"

"Are you listening to yourself, Aiden? You'll forgive her? What right do you have to forgive her of anything? I'm betting you walked away and didn't tell her that you didn't care what she might have done...no, I can see by your face that you didn't. If Zane does decide to contact you, which I highly doubt she will, then it will be because she has no other choice."

Aiden watched as Bailey left the room. He hadn't meant to make her mad and, in turn, make Tristan mad too. He'd told them he didn't want to talk about her and look what happened. Damn it, he should have stayed in France. Stalking to the door Aiden stepped out into the darkness. He heard his brother call his name, but ignored him. He wanted to get away before he said anything that he might regret.

~~~

It was nearing dawn when Zane met up with the vamp. It had taken her nearly two hours to hunt down the master in the area and ask for permission to hunt him. The stupid man, David Cane, was "entertaining" and couldn't be pulled away when she showed up at his house. Even with an appointment Zane had waited an extra hour before she went to his bedroom and threw open the door.

"What the fuck do you think you're doing? Get out unless you wish to play. I have things to do that—"

Zane slammed him up against the headboard of his bed so hard she drew blood. With the backing of the Vampire Council she had more rights than she might have as a bounty hunter. She had only notified this master as a courtesy. She didn't need his permission to hunt. She did, however, wait until the men in his bed left before she spoke.

"Listen you dumb fuck-tard, I have an order to terminate. I came to let you know that I was in your area to execute it. If you don't have the common decency to come and speak to me then you tell me. You don't leave me sitting in your fucking parlor while you fuck three men. From now on, if I come into your area you'd better fucking hope I don't accidently kill you while I'm here."

"You can't talk to me like that. I'm the master of this—" His head hit the headboard three more times.

"I just did. Here is your copy of the order." She slammed the paper at his chest. "Stay the fuck out of my way or so help me, I'll come back and I'll be angry then."

Leaving him crumpled on the bed Zane left the room. She hated his type of vamp. The sort that felt that they were owed whatever their subjects gave them whether pleasure or money. Zane had noticed that Master MacManus seemed to have it right. He was well respected and he seemed to be very generous. As yet she had not had to hunt in his realm, which she found something curious about.

The vampire Zane was hunting was a female. She had been hunting humans and using them as cattle. There was more of her kind than not it seemed. Going out into the world and feeding from humans then leaving them with not only their memory of the feeding, but most times not sealing the wounds. The human would die of massive blood loss and wake the authorities to their kind.

The Council tried very hard to keep vampire lure from the humans, and that is where Zane came in.

It was still an hour until dawn when Zane came upon her lair in the cemetery. The vamp was just warding the crypt when Zane stepped into the chamber above her.

She was old, this vamp, and had spent her first years beneath the earth or in such crypts as the one she now occupied. The information Zane had on her said that she also slept during the day in a coffin and not simply in the ground. Once Zane was in the chamber and the wards set she wouldn't be able to leave. If she didn't kill her she would be stuck inside when the vamp woke.

The wall to the lower levels moved easily enough once Zane found it. The small slide behind one of the bricks had been used so much that there was a small indentation that curved like a finger had been pressed into it. The crypt itself was huge. It held a family for several generations starting in the late seventeen hundreds. The lower level and the mechanism that opened it indicated that there may have been a vampire in the family sometime around the time it had been built. Zane waited until the sun crested the top of the hillside, hit the decorative stain glass just over the door, and painted the floor with brilliant colors.

Opening the door made enough noise to wake the dead Zane thought as the door slid to the side. Once she was on the other side of it she had to rely on her other senses as her sight was gone in the blackness. Closing her eyes, she was able to feel where the walls were and when the floor dipped or raised. With her hands full of the silver blade Zane was glad that she didn't have to worry about tripping as she moved lower underground.

Perhaps one hundred feet from the door, she felt the vamp move out of her sleep. Another ten feet and Zane knew that she was coming toward her as a small rodent. Zane shifted as well, taking the form of a bat, and waited.

"I know that you are there, little one. Come out and play with me. I have a need for fresh blood. You may as well feed me." Zane shuddered at the sound of her voice, low pitched and full of compulsion.

When the rat was just underneath her Zane shifted into her human form and dropped to the body of the rat. She moved before Zane could capture her. Moving with the speed of a vampire herself Zane leapt to the opposite wall when the vamp revealed herself.

"Alexandria DePaul, you are hereby ordered to death by the Vampire Council for crimes against humanity. I am hereby ordered to terminate your life by removing your head. Do you have anything to say?"

Zane only knew the names of the people she killed for the queen and the Council when the laws of humanity were involved. She hated it; knowing the person's name made her feel connected and she didn't need any more connections to the people who died by her hand than necessary.

"You are going to kill me? I think not, child. I will, however, give you a choice. Would you like to die outright, or would you prefer to die slowly? I prefer slow myself—for my dinner, you see. Your terror makes the blood so hot and spicy." Zane watched her move around her. DePaul was herding her toward the stairs that Zane could feel just to her left. "But if you wish to go quickly, I can do that as well. Remove your throat as I feed upon you. What do *you* say?"

Zane pulled the silver blade out from her ribs and paired it with the one from her back. Both were pure silver and had a razor sharp edge to them. They had also been enchanted by the queen after her trial and sentencing. DePaul laughed when Zane pulled them before her body.

"Bring it on, bitch. You should know that my blood will kill you if taken without my permission and I'm so not giving it to you. So this dancing around is for the birds. I'm really tired and I want to go home. I can feel your weakness and your need to rest. So how about we get this shit over with and you let me kill you?"

The attack was quick. DePaul leapt at Zane's throat, her mouth opened wide. Fangs, stained with blood and sharp as a point, touched Zane's neck but didn't break the skin. But the claws, her claws dug deep into Zane's body. She felt her lung collapse and her kidney burst. Breathing became difficult and she knew that she wasn't going to be able to stand much longer. If she didn't kill this bitch now, Zane knew she was going to cut her to ribbons and she would bleed out.

Zane couldn't raise her arm to remove the vamp's head. Gathering as much of the energy in the small chamber as she could, Zane pushed a blue ball of pure energy into her mouth as DePaul opened it to rip Zane's throat out.

CHAPTER 11

"Well, I'm off to rest. I'll see you guys to—" Pain ripped through him. Aiden could feel his kidney burst within his body. His left lung stopped pumping. The world started to fade as he started to fall to the floor. He could hear his brother shouting at him, screaming at him. Aiden couldn't speak, couldn't think past the pain. Then it just stopped. The pain stopped as quickly as it had hit him. Staying on the floor, he held up his hand and took a cautious and slow breath.

"I'm fine. I'm all right. I don't know what...Zane. Zane is in trouble. I could feel her pain. Someone...no, something...a vampire hurt her. But she's... Christ, she took the pain. She took it from me. I know she did. I have to find her." Aiden got up and nearly fell back to the floor, would have if his brother hadn't been there to catch him. Dizzily he sat in the closest chair and put his head into his hands. He could still feel her pain, but it was if he was feeling it from a long distance.

"You told me you didn't bond with her. How is it possible that you can feel her pain without the bond? Aiden, what's going on?" Tristan sounded worried and pissed.

Aiden chuckled. "I wish I knew. I know she's hurt badly. I don't know how I can feel it. She was with a vampiress in a small room, no, a chamber, underground. I can...she's hurt, damn it. I have to go find her." Suddenly, the room expanded then tightened in a way that seemingly sucked all the air out and then back in.

"You can't. She wouldn't let you help her even if you did find her. Hello, Aiden St. James. My name is Melody. We've not had the pleasure of ever meeting. I'm the Queen of Magic and Zane works for me."

Before Aiden stood a vision. She was dressed in maternity jeans and a man's simple dress shirt. Her large belly looked bigger because of her small frame. Her hair, dark as sin, hung down her back in a riot of curls and tangles. Her face was perfect, dark eyes and sculpted brows. Her nose was small and turned at the end in a perfect aristocratic slope.

Aiden had heard the family talk about her. Even little Emma had. This is the woman who showed his niece the unicorns and dragons. He knew it as soon as she shimmered into the room.

"Why can't I find her? I need to...why did I feel her pain? Is she...fuck, this is stupid. Where is she and how badly is she hurt?"

Grinning, Mel answered him. He didn't like that grin. "She is hurt very badly, but she won't die. I made sure of that. Her body will heal until she is no longer in mortal danger and then she will heal as she normally would. Fast, but not like you would. Not yet at any rate." Mel sat down in one of the kitchen chairs and a basket of fruit appeared in front of her. She pulled out a banana and started peeling it as she continued. "I was as surprised as you were that you could feel her pain. I thought when I told you to ask for a boon from her that you would ask her to mate with you. I can see now that you didn't. Mate with her, I mean."

"You spoke to me that day? Why? What business is it of yours if she mates with me or not. I know who you are, but what does that have to do with Zane?"

"Aiden, I don't think you should piss her off. Mel has a...she can be—"

"Don't finish that, Bailey. I'm too hormonal to be nice today. As it is, Shamus is already pissed at me too. I just wanted to see what was going on and why he hadn't bonded with her." Mel turned back to him and smiled. This one didn't reach her eyes. "Why haven't you? She is your other half, you know?"

Aiden could feel Mel searching his mind and he let her. When she had found the reason why, Mel didn't seem any happier about it than he had been. He sat back in his chair and waited. She didn't disappoint.

"Why that stupid, stubborn...you know, there are days that I wish I had let her have her wish. All she had to do was tell me what really happened. But oh no, not her. Miss Zulu Alpha Nine had to just take all the blame. I knew she didn't—"

"What did you call her?" Aiden looked sharply at Bailey when she had asked. The pain in her voice was heart-wrenching. Aiden looked at his brother and saw that he had paled as well.

"The first time I met her I asked her what her name was and that's what she said. I remember telling her what a stupid...Bailey? Honey? Tristan, grab her."

Another being shimmered into the room and put his arms around Mel. Shamus, Mel's mate and the king, Aiden thought as he followed his brother into the living room. Bailey was telling him to put her down. But both men had seen her nearly pass out and Aiden was glad Tristan didn't listen to his mate.

"I'm sorry, Bailey. I never meant for you to find out this way. Me and my big mouth. I knew about the other lab, but didn't put the two of them together until recently," Mel said as she held Bailey's hand.

"Then it's true. She's like me. We weren't the...Griff and I looked. For years we looked for another lab. But we weren't the first, were we? We were the last. Oh that poor girl. How long...how long as it been, Mel?"

"Zane is about seventy years old, I would guess. She's been working as a part of my elite guard for about fifty years, give or take. I...she was there when the building blew, the lab that is. I was angry with Sherman and I know that I...I wasn't fair to her. There wasn't even much of a trial. I even held it right there in that room covered in blood." Aiden watched as Shamus held his mate to him. "Zane was one of the first ones to be made there. I felt the magic one day and I couldn't get there until everyone was dead. I came inside and she refused to tell me who was there, who did those things... Some of those beings were so mistreated it's no wonder that they did what they did."

"Zane is different than me. More advanced. How is that possible if I was made later, when technology was more advanced?"

"They would have had to start over with your works at the lab. She destroyed everything when she blew the building. Computers weren't...they were still doing things on paper then and she just destroyed it all. You're right. She is more advanced than you. The things she can do, it's amazing." Aiden watched Mel shudder as she spoke. Apparently, everything she could do wasn't so nice.

"But that doesn't explain my bond. How could I feel her pain so sharply? I took her blood only—wait! She did take mine. But it was only a drop. She said it was to communicate with me."

Aiden thought about her panther and how she had hit him. He could still feel her jaws clamped around his neck and unconsciously rubbed his hands over his throat. She could have killed him so easily.

"I honestly don't know much about her. I can read her mind, but it is so complicated that it takes so much energy to sort through it. I think she can feel me enter and jumbles things up just to throw me off." Aiden looked up at Shamus when he snorted. "Aiden, meet my mate Shamus. He's an ass."

"Hello. I'm Aiden St. James." Aiden shook his hand. "Why do you laugh? What do you know about her?"

Shamus shrugged. "Have you met Tess? She and Zane could fill an entire book on how to get on Mellie's last nerve. Tess is a good friend of mine, but when I see her coming to the castle to talk to Mellie I run the other way. She and Mel can be very volatile. Don't get me wrong, it's hilarious, but dangerous when they start using their magic." Shamus shrugged again, this time with a huge smile. "Zane is the same way. I run, but I love to hear them go at one another."

Aiden stood up. He needed to retire. He could already feel the sun beating on him. He looked at his brother and knew he was feeling the same effects. But Aiden was no closer to finding Zane than he had been before. As soon as he turned to ask, Mel answered him.

"She'll be at her lair. Her body returns there as soon as she loses consciousness. And before you ask, no, I don't know where it is. I couldn't find it if I tried. It was part of her sentence. She would be available when I called, but her personal life was her own and I could never interfere."

"But aren't you? I mean, this whole mate business. Isn't that interfering?" Aiden asked quietly.

"No. You are her mate. I didn't have anything to do with that. As soon as I found that out, I...she...I found out something recently. I think...I believe that my ex-mate Sherman is part of her DNA. I think that Sherman was responsible for her magic and for the labs. I think he may have taken some of the people from the future back in time to create a superior race of immortal beings for an army to take over the world, the human world. I feel...had I listened to my heart and not my head...without my magic when..." Shamus picked Mel up and nodded to them all before they both shimmered from the room.

"Mother fuck, Shermie is back." Although Aiden had a vague idea who he was, he was thinking Bailey might be right in her assessment of the situation.

~~~

Zane woke in her lair. She could hardly move. Her body was torn up and she was still breathing painfully. While she had slept her body had repaired her kidney and her lung, but the other wounds, the deep cuts and tears in her tissue and muscles, would take a lot longer. Her weapons were also back in place. Groaning, she rolled to her side and started to rise when she felt someone touch her mind.

"You need to mind your own fucking council, woman. I'm tired of working around you and your kind. I have things I've set into motion and you're fucking them up. What will it take to make you stop listening to the Queen of Magick?"

Zane didn't answer but followed his connection back. She could find him now, the man who threatened her. Simon Sinclair.

He was also the one who attacked the master vamp. Touching his mind, she also knew what he was up to. He wanted Sara MacManus. Not just wanted, but was obsessed with her and the realm in which she lived.

"I'm speaking to you, girl. You will answer me. What will it take to make you leave this area never to return? I have plenty of money, and will have much more soon, very soon if you mind your own council."

"And what makes you think I need money? I've everything I have right here, thank you very much. Whatever you want with the queen is none of my concern. I work for her, we aren't friendly. So go bother someone else and leave me be."

Zane put him to the back of her mind. He didn't know who she was, he'd not said her name. There was power in a person's name and she had his. She reached out to the one person she knew would do something with the information. Zane believed he'd do anything to keep his mate safe.

"Master? I've information for you. A being just contacted me to leave the area. He is after your mate and your realm. I can't tell you his name without the permission of the queen. He is the one who shot your home."

Zane could tell he was shocked. First, because she contacted him through a mental link without them exchanging blood and secondly, because of the information itself. She could feel him choosing his words carefully. It made her smile that he didn't want to piss her off.

"And you know this how? Am I to assume that he asked you for something and that you didn't give it to him? And why would I have to ask Mel for information that you have that I need?" Aaron asked her. Zane could hear the suspicion in his voice even through the link.

"Talk to the queen. I'm sure she'll have no problem telling you anything you want to know about why I can't help you. You should also know that he doesn't know your name, or that of your mate. In the future, don't talk to anyone unless they first say your name. Both of you."

"Why? I have...ah, power. He can't hurt me without my name. Or at least that's the assumption. Thank you, my dear. I'm indebted to you."

"Just take care of the babe, master. I've no need of another death upon my soul." Zane didn't either. After doing this for as long as she had, there were many more than she wanted to account for.

Moving as slowly as she could Zane went into her bathroom, thankful for the weekend as she could laze about the house. Peeling off her torn t-shirt and pants, she looked at herself in the mirror.

Bruises and lacerations covered her body. Her legs were black and blue from her hips to her ankles. There was a long gash in her left thigh that still bled and another on her right calf. She didn't remember what had put them there, but she knew they were fresh. The wound on her back where her kidney had been injured was black and at least a foot square in color. There were smaller cuts there as well. Not as bad as on her legs, but no less painful. The tear on her chest just below her breast was eight inches long and needed stitches. Her arms were also black and blue, but the cuts there were superficial. Her jaw was bruised and her left eye was swollen completely shut. She would need more stitches in both of those areas as well. Not wanting to see anything else, she turned off the light and stepped into the steamy heat of the shower.

Zane's night vision was excellent, so when the blood and grime began sluicing from her body she could see the river of redness as it circled around the drain.

Washing her hair Zane could feel several large and smaller bumps and cuts here and there. Her fingers found several of them and had her wincing from the pain. When she was finished scrubbing she let the hot water soothe her broken and battered body. She thought about the man, Aiden, and how he had received her pain.

Zane didn't know why that had happened, and as soon as she'd realized that he'd felt it she'd blocked him. That had taken a great deal of energy to do, but she saw no reason for both of them to hurt like hell. Wondering if she could see if he had been bruised as well, she decided to touch him when she left her lair to find out. That was when she realized she had no idea of the time, only that it was nearing sunset.

Pulling out her ever present black leather pants and t-shirt and pulling them on, Zane went through the tunnel to go to the house she owned. The shower gave her a boost of energy. Not a lot, but more than she'd had. It took her twenty minutes to walk the three mile pathway to her house instead of the normal five. She was drained and hurting again by the time she got there. Opening the back door with a small burst of energy she didn't have, she entered the kitchen and reached for her medical kit immediately. It was under the sink. Aiden was standing in the doorway to the outside when she stood and turned.

"You have to allow me entrance or I can't come in. And I'd prefer to talk to you inside, not standing on the porch," he said in way of greeting.

"How about we start you off out there and you work on allowing yourself inside? And while you say your piece I'm going to work on a few cuts."

CHAPTER 12

Aiden watched as Zane put the first aid kit on the small table. Then she unsnapped her black jeans. He nearly swallowed his tongue when he realized she planned to take them off while he watched. Then his breath caught when he saw what they'd been hiding.

"Christ! How the hell are you even upright? You look...our kidneys...your kidney had been damaged from the blow you took there. Let me in, Zane. I want to help you."

Aiden didn't think she would, so he wasn't surprised when she didn't. He realized his beast was rising when he saw her tense up.

"Say your piece, Mr. St. James. I have to finish here and go feed yet tonight. I still have a report to file and other things that I can't put off. And control your monster. He is bringing mine to the surface."

Aiden watched as she took a white towel and laid it across the opposite chair from where she sat. He had to look away or he'd never get his other self under control.

The kitchen was done in deep blues and whites; the appliances were all a brushed stainless steel. White tiles surrounded the long sink and on the floor. The counter top looked to be granite. There was none of the normal smaller appliances on the counter, no coffee pot, toaster, or blender. There was a microwave. The table and chairs looked new, the table top bare of any placemats and salt or pepper. Aiden looked back at the woman sitting on one of the chairs when she spoke.

"It's an illusion. I'm sure you put one up as well. To make people, humans, believe you are just like them. There's a TV in the other room that's never been turned on and furniture that I've never sat on. There's a bed in one of the rooms on the upper levels that is supposed to be one of the finest made. Yet I sleep far from here in a lair deep underground. Why are you here?"

The question startled him. "I came to see how you are. I felt your pain and I wanted to make sure you were all right. See if you needed anything."

Zane's laugh was bitter and harsh. "I'm just peachy, as you can see. I won't die, no matter how much I try. If you've found this house then you've spoken to her majesty."

There was a good deal of venom in the last word. Aiden would have had to be deaf not to hear it. He wondered at it, but said nothing.

"I did speak to the queen, but I found your home from having someone search for me. Pete, she works with the Brotherhood of the Gray. She found it. She said it was clever of you to use 'Allider Zandson,' by the way. If you hadn't told me your name that day, we might not have figured it out."

Aiden watched as she knotted off the thread at the wound in her thigh. When she moved to the other one in her calf, she hesitated. This one looked deeper than the one on her upper leg and the blood seeped still. He felt his fangs react to the sight of blood.

"You might as well come in. There's fresh blood in the fridge. Your hunger is beating at me and I can't concentrate." She was trying to bring her calf closer to her when she continued. "The queen had a lot to say, I'm sure. All of it is true. She and I don't get along."

Aiden opened the refrigerator and pulled out a bag of whole blood. It was from the local blood bank, the label said. He shook it as he walked to the microwave. He much preferred his blood fresher, as in directly from the source, but he didn't want to leave her just yet.

"All she said was you and she have a history." Her snort made him smile. "And that you work for her. She also pointed out that I should use my favor to make you bond with me."

Aiden waited for the fireworks or, at the very least, shouting. But he was disappointed. He'd talked to Mel about the trade thing. She'd wondered for several seconds before she remembered.

"Sherman, my supposed mate, never got that part right. He was the one that would make a person trade for a boon no matter what it was for. He was incredibly stupid, to say the least. He must have told her how it worked in his mind. She wouldn't know any better."

"So you're not going to tell her?" Aiden didn't think it was all that honest, but didn't know.

"If I do then you have nothing to bargain with her for. If she continues to believe that's how it works then we both get what we want. I'm sure that in the end you'll see how it will help you."

Her smile made him nervous and he nearly asked her about it. But there was something holy scary about the queen. For all her sweet and beautiful face, she, he knew, would do whatever it took. To do anything.

When the microwave dinged he poured the blood into two glasses and sat them on the table with her. Picking up her ankle he sat in the chair she was resting her injured leg on and pulled it into his lap.

"You surprised me. Pissed me off too, but surprised me more. Wipe this down and I'll stitch it closed." As she wiped the blood away like he'd asked, he started pulling the needle through her muscled calf.

"I could do this. I don't need your—"

"Yes you do. Now shut up and listen. I'm not going to do it, the bonding with you. I just said she told me I should. I think you deserve more than that and frankly, so do I." Aiden finished the neat row of stitches and took the bloodied towel from her. He could feel her anger and was sure she was letting him. He couldn't feel her pain, though, he was sure she was hurting. He looked up at her.

"Why? Why would you go against the wishes of the queen when it's something you want as well? If it's to impress me, it's not working. I'm pretty stubborn."

Aiden threw back his head and laughed. "I would say that's an understatement. I have a feeling you're very stubborn. Let me take care of your other wounds. I believe you have one on your chest too."

Zane stared at him for several seconds before she stood. When she swayed, he put his hands on her hips to hold her up. Hot soft skin filled his hands. When Zane leaned back against his chest, it was all he could do not to bury his nose in her neck. Her scent filled his senses and pulled him hard. His cock, already aching, seemed to expand and lengthen in his jeans. A small groan escaped his throat before he could stop it. When she went to pull away he growled deep.

"You should leave. Now. I've got things to do tonight. And you...you'd be in my way."

Leaving was probably a good idea. Very good idea as a matter of fact, but he needed to prove to her that he could be around her without taking her. No matter what he really wanted. Even though every fiber of his being wanted him to lean her over the table and take her—hard and fast. He pulled away and stepped back.

"Let me tend to your back and chest first. I want to make sure that you aren't bleeding anymore. I know that you took quite a blow back here and I can see that the one on your front is soaking though your shirt."

Aiden didn't think she'd let him. He thought for sure she was going to toss him out on his ear when she turned and looked at him.

"Why are you doing this? I'm not stupid, you know. I know that you think to sooner or later wear me down and I'll become your whatever. But you won't."

Aiden didn't answer her. He couldn't because she was right. He was hoping to wear her down. Hoping that if he let her think he was charming she would let him claim her as his. He hoped that she would become his mate, his other half, for several lifetimes.

When Zane walked to the door and opened it, Aiden hesitated for several seconds then walked to stand in front of her. Need coiled in his belly. Need for this woman and all that she represented.

"This isn't finished, Zane. I'll be back. You know who you are to me. But what you don't know is how relentless I am when I want something. And I do want you."

Aiden was shocked by the tears that welled in her eyes. More so when they began to fall. When he reached to pull her to him she stopped him with a single word.

"Don't."

And he almost didn't. Pulling her close, he gave her a brief kiss on her mouth then thumbed the tears away with his left thumb. Before she could say anything, he left. When the door closed softly behind him he closed his eyes and raised his face to the night sky. Shifting quickly into his large eagle, Aiden took to the night.

~~~

Zane knew when Aiden left her area. The tight ball of nerves loosened in her belly and the strain in her shoulders loosened as well. Taking her first deep breath since he showed up, Zane picked up their untouched glasses and dumped them into the sink.

Setting them on the counter, Zane unloaded the dishwasher and laid the clean dishes to the left of the sink. Opening the cabinets, she began pulling down dishes and arranging them in the washer. Several glasses first, then three bowls, a plate, and even a platter went in. Though Zane wasn't sure what the cleaning lady would think about that in the washer, she wasn't sure. Reaching behind her and beside the stove, Zane put two small pots and a frying pan in. Opening the silverware drawer, she added four spoons, three forks, and a steak knife. Satisfied, Zane shut it up and put the other dishes away.

Reaching into the bag beside the closed back door, Zane took out the most recent newspapers and two magazines and went to the living room with both the still wet glasses that Aiden had filled with blood. Putting one on the coffee table and one on the floor by the fireplace, Zane took the papers, opened them, and dropped them on the floor in several places. Picking up the remote to the television, she pushed it between the seat cushions on the couch along with a section of the paper. Satisfied with this room, she went to the upper levels.

Zane knew what she was doing—stalling. She refused to think about Aiden, and doing the work she was now doing made him seem so less real—at least for the moment. Reaching into the top drawer of the massive dresser Zane pulled out a pair of black leather pants and pulled them on as she went into the bathroom to drop a towel and smear toothpaste on the sink.

Aiden had kissed her. No matter how much she prepared the house for the cleaning lady, that single thought kept circling in her head. Even as she mussed the bed and tossed sheets to the floor, she couldn't quite work her head around that single thought.

When Zane made her way back to the kitchen she thought about how he'd told her what the queen had wanted and the fact that he'd refused her. Why, she wondered? Going to the basement door and pushing the panel to the right, Zane stepped into the dark hidden tunnel.

Zane started down the stairs after she secured the door. Halfway to the opening into the night, she felt the first stirrings of someone trying to touch her mind. She stilled, becoming so stiff she looked like a statue standing in the deep path.

Simon Sinclair again. This time he was pushing hard to get into her mind. Giving him a little more information to play with, she moved into his mind as well. Less intrusive and much easier, Zane searched for something to tell her what he really wanted with her.

His mind was a jumble of half thought and stupid ideas. It took her several seconds to find out three things. One, he'd never met the MacManuses. His obsession with Sara stemmed from her magic and not her and her ability to breed. Secondly, he was a vampire and wolf mix, and lastly, he was running with a little girl. Emma St. James.

As soon as she figured out who the child belonged to, her pager vibrated against her hip. Zane was in no shape to go after the kid, but shifted and raced back to her house to call in. When she was at the paneled door she felt the movement of someone on the other side. Not bothering to shift back fully, Zane flexed her hand until she had fingers and pressed the panel open. Easing the doorway open, Zane waited until the person walked to this side of the other room before stepping into the kitchen. She waited for the person to move toward her again. She only had the one chance and she refused to lose it. When the being was just on the other side of the open doorway Zane pounced at him.

Bradley Wolfe nearly got his head removed and would have too if Zane had not recognized him from the bar. As he tumbled to the floor with her weight thrown against him he never shifted or retaliated, but waited for her to make the first move. Zane thought he was smarter than he looked.

CHAPTER 13

Bradley waited. He wasn't just afraid of her, but terrified. He was an alpha of his own kind, but she was a cat and not wolf. And she was fucking huge. He knew he could probably kill her, his wolf was actually snarling at him to do so, but he needed help. When she shifted to human he'd never been so happy in his life.

"What the fuck do you think you're doing here? I could have killed you, you moronic jackass. Ever hear of break and—"

The back door flew open and crashed against the wall, breaking glass and panes in it. Bradley found himself being tossed against the wall this time. For the second time in five minutes someone was trying to kill him. Aiden wasn't as easy to calm either.

Aiden's mate had been challenged. And she had probably been scared. Bradley knew just how he felt. If anyone had done anything like he'd done to his mate, Bradley knew that he'd kill them.

Bradley looked into the vampire's blood red eyes and tried to remain calm. "Your brother sent me here to find Zane and you. Someone has taken Emma. I've come to ask Zane to help find her."

"Damn it, Aiden! Look what you did to this door. You're fucking paying for it. And to have this mess cleaned up."

Bradley couldn't figure out why she was going on about that when a child was missing, but Aiden suddenly seemed to snap out of it. She was distracting him, calming his beast. When Aiden let

Bradley go, he leaned back against the cabinet even as his own mate reached out to him.

"You do know how to stir up trouble, don't you? I told you to call her. I knew this was going to happen, didn't I tell you that?"

Bradley bristled. He didn't need her to start in on him too. He looked over at the couple standing arguing about the door and smiled. Damn but they were a furious pair.

"Hush, woman. I won't bring you home any apple dumplings if you don't behave. I have it on good authority that Cade has been baking since she and Kyle came into town."

That shut her up. Bradley cleared his throat as the two in front of him seemed to have forgotten about him. He had to clear his throat twice more before they looked at him.

"I'm going after the kid. You stay here and guard the door since you broke it. And when the repair—"

"She's my niece and I'm going. You stay here and guard the door. You're too hurt to go out anyway. Just tell me what you know." Bradley thought Zane was going to hit Aiden, but wisely shut up.

Just when they looked to start on each other again Bradley spoke up. "I have a pack pup that'll stay with the door. I'll pay for the repair. Just please, for the love of all that's holy, just stop bickering at each other! Christ, you act like you hate each other."

Zane glared at him before she spoke. "I'm going as a cat. If you can keep up then you can go." She turned to Bradley. "If you let me sip your blood, I'll—"

The growl emanating from Aiden had his wolf stir. Mates could be dangerous. Especially this close to another alpha. But Zane didn't get it or, more than likely, didn't care.

"Oh grow up, you oversized ape. When we need your pack I'll contact you. Deal?"

Bradley looked at Aiden. He knew what the vamp was going through. But Zane was right; she had to take his blood. She could take his blood without causing a conflict with Aaron, Aiden's master. At Aiden's nod and Zane's eye roll, Bradley held out his finger for her to prick. A quick swipe of her tongue and she shifted. A graceful move, from human to panther in an instant. Aiden shifted as well. His panther was twice that of Zane's, but both were muscled and dangerous. When Zane touched his mind she was already out the broken door with Aiden looping after her.

"There's a pager on the counter I left for you. Call the number on the screen and tell him I'm engaged. If he asks you to verify you have to say, 'the rain in Spain falls mainly in the plains.' Tell him what I'm doing and that I search."

"Are you kidding me? If he asks me to say that with an accent, you'll pay." Bradley could feel her laughter as he dialed. He recognized the voice at the other end immediately. "Griff?"

"Yes, my lord. How are you this fine evening? Well I hope."

Bradley thought this night couldn't get any more surreal. "Fine. And yourself? Zane asked me to call this number and tell you she was engaged."

Laughter greeted him. Bradley sat in one of the kitchen chairs and waited. He didn't have long.

"The child? She goes for it then. Good. The family is frantic and has called the queen. I will need for you to verify, sire. It is important."

Bradley repeated the line from one of his favorite movies and wondered how Audrey Hepburn would feel about its current usage. Then realized it was as good as any in its password usage.

When the two of them hung up Bradley called his friend and master of this vampire realm, Aaron. And within a few minutes, the two men were sitting in the living room enjoying Zane's big screen television, confident in the two people who were searching for the small child.

~~~

Aiden followed Zane as she raced through the woods. She was beautiful as a woman, but as a panther, she was magnificent. Even as a matched panther, he wanted to cover her. But he had to find Emma.

"Do you know who has her and why? My brother Tristan is pounding against my head for information. Any information."

"I'm going to have to wait on the queen to give me permission to give him anything. She isn't...I'm not able to contact her. She has to contact me first," Zane whispered back to him.

Aiden frowned at that. She could reach anyone she wanted with just a drop of blood, but she couldn't contact the queen. That didn't make sense to him.

"Why not? Why can't you contact her? You should have taken her blood long before now, I would think."

Aiden felt her anger. It was hot and sharp. For some reason the scent of her anger aroused him and he could feel his beast, the vampire, respond to it.

"Is sex all you ever think about? Christ! I can't contact her anymore because I...because I was a bit of a nuisance when she first ordered me to go work for her. Now if I try, she...she can be a real bitch when she wants to be."

Aiden found himself smiling at that. That was twice now that people had warned him about the queen. Remembering that she had contacted him once before Aiden visualized her and reached for her. He didn't expect it to work. Vampires could only contact through blood. It was a more intimate path for mates, but he tried anyway.

"Hello, Aiden. Yes, I'm aware of what's going on. And I'll talk to my employee in a bit. You should know that the man who has your niece is the one who shot up your master's home. I'm sure that Zane knows it already. If you would just mate with her then you'd—"

"No. She is going to have a choice in this. I'm sorry, my lady, but I'll give her this for as long as I can. I believe it is important to her. To us."

"Well, don't wait too long, Aiden. I don't like to see her like this. Did she tell you why she works for me?" Aiden could feel her frustration. *"No, don't answer that. She wouldn't unless I let her. I'll contact her, but Aiden? You need to at least exchange blood with her. It's important."*

Aiden could feel her move out of his mind, but not completely. There was a small touch of her still there that he'd never felt before. He was about to speak to Zane about it when she stopped suddenly.

"I don't know the little girl's scent. But I know that Sinclair has been this way. Can you scent her?"

Aiden raised his head and struck out his tongue to hopefully pull more of her in. Just as he was about to say he couldn't, he found her.

"Yes. I can smell her this way. I can—"

"Wait! Aiden, it's a trap. Don't go that way. She isn't that way. Sinclair went this way."

Aiden turned to look at Zane. *"I know my own niece and she is this way. I've been around her a lot longer than you, Zane. I think I'd know a trap if I saw one."*

Zane's anger hit him again. This time, he felt it was unjustified. *"Oh! So just because you're as old as rock and as thick-headed as one, you are naturally right? I'm telling you it's a trap. If you go that way, I'm leaving your sorry ass there."*

"And I'm telling you we're going this way. Come on. We have to get her back. It's nearly dawn." Aiden decided to ignore the rock and his head reference. She was hurt and obviously in a great deal of pain.

Aiden didn't turn to see if Zane followed, confident in his ability to make her listen to him. He loped over a felled tree just as the first dart hit him. Then another. He felt his body stagger even as three more darts hit him. His last thought before he fell to the ground was that he was never going to live this down.

CHAPTER 14

Zane knew the exact moment that Aiden fell. She didn't turn back to get him, but reached into the earth and asked it to pull him to safety. The part of her that was fae worked to save the arrogant idiot and she could feel the soil respond to her request. No one would find him either.

Zane could almost see the trail that Sinclair tried to hide. That was actually what Zane was planning to follow. She knew that is where the little girl would be. She came upon the child tied to a tree as soon as she cleared the forest. Zane stayed her cat and circled the area several times looking for the secondary trap. She had already spotted the first one. It was tripwires set all over the ground.

All around the tree in different intervals were small incendiary devices attached to branches and trees ready to trip if she made a wrong move. She could see them well enough, almost too well. The little girl crying was getting to her so Zane shifted to try and calm her.

"Look, kid, I need to try and get you out of this. My name is Zane. I know your parents. They sent me. Your Uncle Aiden too. I have to figure this out so I can get you. Understand?" The kid nodded, the gag in her mouth preventing her from speaking. "See the wires all along the ground? They'll blow if I trip them. But I think there's something more. Do you know what else he did to stop me from getting over there?"

The kid looked up with her eyes. That's when Zane noticed the wire around her throat—a garrote. Zane looked up into the tree and saw the pulley system then. Moving to around the back again Zane had it figured out.

"Okay, kid, here's the deal. The wire around your neck is to remove your head if I try and cut it. But if I cut it, then the one around your wrists will sever your hands. My first instinct would have been to cut the one at your throat. But your wrists slit would mean an instant death." Zane realized she was scaring the kid and tried to think of how to keep her from crying again. "Don't, okay? I've got it. You're not gonna lose any parts. Just stop fu...stop crying, okay?"

Shifting back to panther, because it was easy for her to hold the shape as she was familiar with her, Zane leapt over four of the trip wires. As the cat, she could also jump further. Leaping the last five feet Zane moved slowly toward the kid as she shifted. "I'm not going to take your gag off yet. But I will cut a slit in the tape for you to talk. Don't make me regret doing it, okay? I have to think." Pulling the blade at her ankle, Zane knelt down in front of the little girl. "Pull your tongue all the way back in your mouth. Then open your lips as wide as you can for me." When Emma did that, Zane cut a slit in the tape for her.

"You're very rude, did you know that? Momma said people should say 'please' and 'thank you.' You never say either."

"Well, this isn't a tea party, kid, so we do it my way. Am I going to have to tape your mouth back up? Good. What were you doing when he snatched you anyway?" Zane walked around the tree. "You should be more careful. There are a lot of sick people out there."

"I was in my bed. I want my momma. Can't you just let me go, please? I need to pee and I want to go home."

The wire around Emma's wrist was cutting her. Blood was beginning to trickle down her small wrists. The lead wire went up the tree then around her throat. If Zane cut the one around Emma's throat, the weight—in this case, a huge boulder—would drop and take both her hands off. If Zane cut the one around her wrist, the weight would still fall and cut through her throat. Emma was never meant to live.

Zane had to do something about the counter weight. Going behind the tree, this time to shift, Zane turned into a small jay. Going to the branch just above the boulder, she could now see what she wanted. Flying down to the ground, she landed again behind the tree and shifted to human. It was extremely difficult to hold the shape of something so small and Zane's exhausted body couldn't hold it that well anyway.

"Okay, kid. This is what we're going to do. I have to cut the boulder down. It's going to come down really fast so I need you not to move. If you move when I have to come down fast to catch it, I might trip over you, then you and I both are screwed. I need to know where you are all the time. Get it? If you do what I tell you, you'll be fine and I can get you home."

"I'm afraid. What if you fall anyway? Then I'll be smashed and you won't tell my momma where I am."

"I'm sorry, kid. I don't know any other way. We have to do it now. I still have to save your stupid uncle's butt yet."

"My Uncle Aiden is not stupid. You should be nice to people. I'm nice." Zane raised a brow at that. "Okay. I'll sit really still. But if you get me dead, I'm not going to like you very much."

Zane decided she liked this kid. She had a smart mouth and knew what she wanted. Zane wanted to tell her that if anything happened to her she'd not like herself much either, but decided this wasn't the time.

Shifting to the bird Zane went to just above the boulder then shifted back again. Exhaustion was weighing heavily on her. She was losing blood, but she knew that she was Emma's only chance. Her plan was to cut the wire and then materialize below to catch it. She knew that all the shifting was going to make her slower so she would cut through the wire just enough so that she had a few extra seconds.

"Okay, kid. Steady now. Okay?"

"My name is Emma, not kid. And you be careful too, Miss Zane." She watched as Emma stiffened her legs. "Okay, I'm ready."

Taking a deep breath and closing out everything around her Zane cut through the wire. She just managed to catch the larger boulder a few inches from the child's head. Tossing it to the side, Zane dropped to her knees. Her left wrist was broken and from her shoulder all the way down each arm was cut and beginning to bruise. The wound in her thigh and calf were open again and the wound in her chest was bleeding badly. Zane wanted to drop, but she still had to get the kid back over the wires and home yet.

"Kid...Emma, you okay?" Zane knew her voice was low, but Emma must have heard.

"Yes. But you look awful. Thank you for saving me. Can I go home now?"

Zane cut the wires from her. "Just give me a minute, okay?" Zane sat down hard. There wasn't any way she could transport them both. "I have to carry you home. Will the big cat scare you?"

Emma whimpered slightly. Zane knew she would be scared. Her panther was huge, especially to a kid. Reaching into Emma's mind to compel her not to be afraid, Zane found the memory of her uncle's birthday gift.

"Okay, kid. But if you tell anyone I did this I'll never speak to you again." Zane shifted into the beautiful carousel horse. The horse was a bright white with a mane of bright green and red hair. Her hooves were golden and the saddle a dark blood red. Emma scrambled on her back when Zane dropped down for her.

Taking several small steps to try and control the pain of running on a broken leg, Zane just managed to leap over the trip wires. Sending out a compulsion to keep other animals away until she could return to disarm it Zane turned to take Emma home.

Zane nearly fell over when she tried to take another step after the jump. Everything, every part of her, was screaming in pain. But suddenly Emma laughed. A delighted child's laugh then she leaned down and kissed Zane on her long neck.

Zane knew then that she'd get the kid home if it killed her. She was taking her to the master's house as he was the closest. It would take them about thirty minutes to get there, so she reached out to the master.

"I have the child. I'm bringing her to you. I still have to go and get Aiden to shelter."

"Thank goodness. Is she all right? I'm telling her parents now. Tristan is frantic with worry about his brother."

"Yes, she's fine—cuts and bruises, but nothing that won't heal quickly. Aiden is hidden from the man who drugged him. He is below the ground. I'll take him...I'm injured and I can't make this trip again. I can get him to safety and I know he'll be well if you would allow me this. Could you...the queen will... I can't work again. Not until I heal more. Do you think, sire, that you could—"

"You have done so much for me, for my Kiss, Zane. Let me worry about the queen. Thank you, Allison Zander. I owe you...my Kiss owes you a great deal."

When Zane stopped in front of the mansion Tristan, Bailey, Sara, and Aaron came out to greet her and take the child. Emma was in her mother's arms almost immediately. With the burden of the kid off her, Zane shifted again. She nearly fell, and would have too if Sara had not caught her.

"You need to feed. Here, take mine. It's powerful and will sustain you quickly." When Zane backed away, Sara advanced toward her. "Don't be a stubborn ass, Allison, take the damned blood."

"No. Your blood would poison me. And for as much as I would normally relish the consequences, the queen has made it impossible for me to die. I have to go." Zane turned to Emma. "Kid, you did all right."

Shifting, Zane went to get Aiden to shelter. The sun was minutes from its peak. So putting on some extra speed, expending energy that she didn't really have and could ill afford, Zane made it to where his body was buried beneath the vines and earth.

Zane shifted back to her human form for what she knew would be the last time until she could rest and heal. She wrapped her body around his and took them both to her lair. She had just managed to get them into the dark room when her body simply shut down. She couldn't even summon the energy to get them to the bed, but on the floor near it. Her last thought before blackness claimed her was that he was going to be sore from this.

~~~

Aiden woke to a strange place. He tried to remember what had happened that would have had him on the floor then remembered the darts hitting his body as a panther. Rolling to his side he landed on another person. He knew immediately it was Zane.

Summoning lights, the room glowed with hundreds of candle lights shimmering off the darkened walls. Looking around her lair he wondered again why they were on the floor and not the huge bed just beyond them.

Standing up, Aiden leaned down, pulled her into his arms, took her to the bed, and gently laid her down. Finding a bedside lamp, he turned it on. His breath caught at the sight of her.

Blood was smeared all over her face. Her eyes, closed, had dark circles beneath them. Bruises covered her jaw and her cheek. Dried blood ran along her neck from her ear. Her right wrist was broken and when he gently touched it she whimpered in her sleep. Commanding her into a deeper rest, Aiden set the bones. The wound in her chest was open, and sliding off the edge of her bed, he went to see if he could find a first aid kit. Finding nothing more than a band aid and some peroxide, he went back to the bedroom.

Aiden tried to think what to do. He could heal her with his blood, but she would be pissed. He could call Mel to her, but knew that Zane would be even more pissed. Smiling, he leaned into the bed near her ear. "Zane, you're my mate, and as such I need to heal you. If you don't have a problem with me providing for you just remain quiet." Aiden grinned again. "Okay then." Putting his wrist to his mouth he bit deep to bring his blood flowing quickly. Pressing it to her mouth, he tilted her head back and whispered to her. As soon as her mouth filled, she swallowed.

Watching her feed from him made his cock swell with need. Trying for something to distract him, anything, Aiden reached for his brother.

"Christ! I've been worried sick. Where are you? Aaron told us yesterday that Zane was getting you to safety, then nothing. For all we knew, you both could have been killed."

"Tristan, Zane is my mate. I don't know what to do about her. She saved Emma, didn't she?"

"Yes. Emma said she's rude and doesn't say 'please' and 'thank you,' but she liked her."

Aiden chuckled at that. That sounded just like both of them. He wished he could have seen them together. He looked down at Zane. He could see her being rude to Emma. But she had saved her too.

"Zane was hurt. Her wrist was broken and there are bruises all over her. Her wounds are...I'm feeding her. She's going to be really mad at me when she wakes."

Aiden could feel his brother's laughter. *"I believe, brother dear, that is a gross understatement on your part. I believe you might have been a bit luckier with the man who tried to kill you."*

Aiden thought his brother might be correct. *"She knew more than me about what was going on. I walked right into a trap. I'm not even sure how I got back here."*

"Aaron said that she had the earth cover you from whoever it was that drugged you. When she dropped off Emma at the master's she looked exhausted. Sara tried to feed her but..."

Aiden knew whatever had happened he wasn't going to like. Zane was proving to be more stubborn than even he was. And that was saying a great deal. *"But what? Why didn't she...is it because Sara is pregnant? She'd told Sara that when she was there when the master's house had been shot."*

"Sara's pregnant? Damn! No, Zane said that Sara's blood would poison her. Aiden, she also said that while it would make her sick, death was being denied her by the queen. Do you know what that's about?"

Aiden glanced at the woman now stirring on the bed. When she sat up and glared at him he knew without a doubt she was going to make him pay for feeding her. He answered his brother before closing the connection. *"No, but I intend to find out. Kiss Emma for me, brother dear. I'll contact you later."*

Aiden shifted around so that he was facing Zane, but just far enough away that he had time to brace for whatever she threw his way. And he had no doubt she would throw something. "How are you feeling, Allison? My brother said Emma is fine." Aiden shifted on his feet slightly when she stood up.

He groaned when she started removing her t-shirt. When it came up over her head and bared her back he saw the sword. When he took a step forward to touch it, touch her, he stopped when she turned and suddenly threw a knife.

"You stay the fuck away from me, you bastard."

Aiden could barely take his eyes from the quivering knife that landed between his feet. It landed dead center with the blade a good inch in the polished wood floor.

"Allison, you were—"

"You had no right! I saved you. I brought you here to save you and this is how you repay me? By feeding me your blood? I told you no!"

"I have every right," Aiden shouted back at her. "Damn it, you were hurt, bleeding. I couldn't sit by and let you suffer needlessly."

When she started forward he braced himself for whatever she was planning. When she reached down and pulled the blade from the floor he thought for a second she was going to bury it in his chest. But before she could do anything he noticed her bared breasts.

CHAPTER 15

Zane looked down at her breasts when Aiden continued to stare at her. Cupping her hands around them, trying to hide them from his view, had him stepping to her.

"Don't, Allison. Let me...Christ, but you're beautiful." His voice was husky and low. It did things to her body she'd not felt in...well, never before.

When he cupped his hands over hers and lifted them with his her breath caught. Then when he smoothed his thumbs over the top swell of her she closed her eyes, not wanting him to see the affect he was having on her. But she couldn't stop the small moan when he ran his tongue along the same path.

Aiden's tongue was hot and wet as he moved it along her other breast. When he gently moved her hands away and filled his with her breasts, Zane felt the ground tilt beneath her.

"Please...I...please, Aiden." Zane hated to beg, but she needed more, more of what he was doing to her and more of what she was sure he could do to her.

Aiden seemed to understand and picked her up by cupping her ass in his hands and lifting her up so that her breasts were right at his mouth. As soon as her back touched the wall behind her he pulled her nipple deep into his mouth. Every nerve in her body felt him. Wrapping her legs around his waist Zane buried her fingers in his hair and held him to her.

"Baby, if you're going to stop me, now would be the time. If not, I'm going to move us to that big bed and fuck you until we can't move. Tell me, Allison, tell me you want me as much as I want you."

Zane's hissed "yes" had her flat on the bed quick. His mouth moved up her shoulder even as she moved her hands to the front of his shirt. As soon as she touched it, it disappeared. Aiden pulled back to look at her.

"Nice trick. Can you make us both naked? I need to feel your body beneath mine now. Right now, Allison."

Aiden's pants disappeared next, along with his boxer briefs, shoes, and socks. Zane reached down and cupped his cock in her hand. He was thick and hard. And the small pearl of cum on the tip made her mouth water. Thumbing it off, she brought it to her mouth and suckled it. Aiden growled deep.

"Take them off. Take them off before I tear them from your body," he growled in her neck.

As suddenly as his clothes disappeared, hers did as well. Aiden leaned up on his hands and looked down both their bodies. His cock throbbed with apparent need and even her tight curls were wet with her cream. Aiden leaned further back on his knees. Zane whimpered.

But when he began stroking his cock with his left hand, he entered her with his fingers of his right. Zane could feel her body responding to what he was doing; the in and out motions matched what he was doing to his cock perfectly.

"Aiden, please stop playing with me. Fuck me."

Aiden's smile was pure sin. "So impatient. But so am I. Zane, look at me. I won't bite if you say no. But I'm going to fuck you. Hard. And until you scream. But I won't take you without your permission."

Zane wanted him to. She wanted to feel his fangs sink deep into her throat as he filled her. But she didn't want him hurt if the queen changed her mind or if she granted Zane's wish of being set free.

"Not yet. Please. You need to talk to the queen first. You have to know what I am, who I am, and what I've done."

Aiden leaned forward and, as he covered his mouth with hers, she saw the hurt. She hadn't meant to hurt him. But as soon as she felt his cock at her entrance she forgot everything else for the moment. Scared for the first time in decades, she screamed when he slammed deep into her, breaking through her virginity quickly.

Pain surged through her. Just when she thought she'd scream at him to stop, he pulled up and looked down at her. There was something there, some emotion she'd never seen on a human or vampire before.

"I'm sorry. I didn't think about...are you all right?"

She started to tell him no, then he moved. Zane wasn't stupid. She knew all about sex. When she'd been in the lab they'd made them watch people copulate so that if the time came and they needed to have sex to prove they were human they would know the basics. But nothing, no movies, no films, nothing could have prepared her for the feelings she got when he moved inside of her.

"That feels good. Do it again. Slower this time." When he chuckled, she looked up at Aiden, ready to blast him, but there was that look again. "What's wrong? Am I doing something wrong?"

"No. Christ, no. You feel good. Tell me what else you want from me, Zane." His voice was low, husky, and velvety along her skin.

"Why do I get the feeling that...oh, yes! Please, do that again. Aiden, please, you should...don't stop, please." His laughter this time was smooth and soft.

When he pulled nearly out of her, she could still feel a part of him within her. When he moved deep, his body pressing hard against her, she wrapped her legs around his hips and locked her ankles around him. Aiden growled deep in his chest when Zane wrapped her hands around his shoulders.

His movements were slow, almost measured. She wanted to make him go faster, harder, but this...she was really enjoying this. When he nuzzled her neck she was so close to letting him sink his teeth into her and drink. He moved on before temptation got the better of her. When his mouth moved over her jaw and up to her mouth Zane suckled his lip, worrying it until he pulled back, his lip still in her mouth until it popped free. As his movements got stronger, deeper, and more frantic Zane felt her own body responding to him.

A need of something rippled along her skin, making her instinctively tighten her legs around him. When Aiden palmed her breast and rolled her nipple between his finger and thumb he licked her throat. Her breath caught and her heart went into overdrive. She wanted him to mark her, to take her more than she wanted her next breath.

When Aiden suckled at her vein without breaking the skin it was almost too much. His whispered command sent her over the edge. "Come. Now, Zane. Come."

Her body responded to him as though he was her master and she had no choice. She bowed up off the bed and screamed out his name as wave after wave of pleasure moved through her body. Every time she started to come down he would say something, do something to her that had her reaching that peak again and again. When she was sure that she couldn't take any more Aiden took her higher; his body pounded into hers faster and harder until she felt him stiffen above her. Then with a powerful thrust, he roared out her name, his body taking hers with quick, hard jabs as he filled her with his cum. Over and over he surged into her body until he finally slowed then collapsed atop of her.

As sleep claimed her she knew that she was lost. Aiden would not give up until he had claimed her fully. She needed to speak to the queen before that happened, and it would be soon she was sure. Zane rolled over and felt Aiden pull her closer to him as she closed her eyes.

Zane was used to sleeping very little. Her jobs, the one at the garage and the one she worked for the queen, had her running on both ends. So when she woke only an hour after they'd had sex she wasn't surprised. What she was surprised about was that Aiden wasn't in the bed with her. She reached out to him and discovered that he was in the bedroom down the hall and in the slumber of his kind. Rolling out of his bed Zane tried not to be hurt by his leaving her.

By the time she had a quick shower and materialized in her own lair it was well past noon. She had to get to the garage and call Danny to let him know she was still coming in.

"No problem. I heard through the grapevine that some pretty unicorn saved Tristan and Bailey's kid. Russell said it had to be you. You can shift, right?"

"Yeah, I can shift." Zane decided that someone was going to pay for that 'rumor.' "I can be there in about ten minutes. I have some stuff being delivered there at two for that POS in the back."

"All right. Oh yeah, there is another thing here for you. It's from some place called 'The Kingdom of Sinclair.' Is that some sort of kinky place you order all them leathers from?"

Zane froze. He knew her. Or so he thought. "Who's it addressed to, Danny? Me or the shop?"

"You know, I don't know. Let me check. Hang on."

While he was checking, Zane did something she hadn't done in decades. She reached for the queen. It didn't take her long for her to touch back. *"There's a problem. It could be big, but right now it's just a problem. Someone is trying to get me to overthrow you and give up the MacManuses. With your permission, I'd like to set up a meeting with him and his Mrs."*

"Agreed. If you think it's something bigger than it is, I'd like to…Sara is my cousin and I'd very much like to be there with you when you talk to them. I can be there in an hour." Zane could hear the concern in the queen's voice and tried not to be moved by it.

"I can't do an hour. I have to appear normal since you won't let me be dead. I can be there after three. I owe Danny."

"Zane, this is much more important than some stupid job. I want you to—"

"You can 'want' all you care to. I'll be there after three. If you want to go and upset them now, be my guest." Zane closed the connection.

It was getting harder and harder for her to speak to the queen. Zane knew it had a lot to do with this mate thing with Aiden, but not all. Zane was tired. Not just tired, but worn down, and she just wanted to end it. When Danny came back on the line she brushed at the tears, refusing to think of them as anything but exhaustion.

"It's to you…well, that's not right either. It says to the Mechanic. I guess I just assumed it was to you. Shall I open it?"

"No!" Zane took a deep breath and tried again. "No. I don't want…Danny, do you trust me?"

"Zane? What the heck is going on? I trust you, but you're starting to scare me a little here. What's in this package? Should I call David and tell him to meet you here?"

If only it were that easy. She'd been compromised, her cover blown. More than that, she'd involved Danny and Russell and whoever else Simon knew she was with. That meant all kinds of people.

"Don't call the police. I need you to put the package outside of the garage and leave it be. I don't…I'm sorry, Danny, but close up and go to Russell. I need to be sure that you and he are safe. It could be nothing, but then again it might not be nothing. I'll call some people and have them protect you. Please?"

"I don't like this. Not one bit. I'll close up now, but you have to promise me something in return. All right?"

Zane closed her eyes. Here it came, he was going to tell her that she couldn't come back to work or, worse yet, he was going to tell her not to come around anymore. She leaned her head against the cabinet above the phone and answered him. "All right, Danny. I understand. I didn't mean to bring trouble to you and yours. I'll keep away from—"

"Mother pots, Zane. Why would you…you are to be safe. That's what I want. Good heavens to Betsy, woman, I don't…your friendship means a great deal to Russell and me. I want you to be safe, kiddo. You be careful and come back to us, you hear?"

Zane didn't know what to say. She wasn't even sure she could speak over the large lump in her throat. No one had ever wanted her friendship before much less thought enough of her to tell her to be safe. It took her a full minute before she could answer him. "Yeah, I will. I'll keep in contact. Stay away from the package, Danny, and I'll pick it up later."

Reaching for the queen again, she simply gave her the facts. *"Change of plans. Things have gone from a problem to a FUBAR. I'll meet you at the MacManus' in one hour."*

~~~

Sara sat at the table and just looked at Mel. Seriously looked at her. This went beyond just an announcement, this was scary.

"We have to tell Bailey. She...Christ, Mel, are you sure? I mean, that would put Sherman plotting against you before we made him pay for...well, from the beginning."

Mel had just told Sara that she was positive that Sherman was the magic behind Zane's power, that he had given some of his DNA to the lab rats he'd had working for him to give her the magic she now had. If that were true then Zane was a true immortal or as close as one could get.

"Yes, so it would seem. I don't know what to tell her. When I first met Zane I was so angry. Not at her, but with Sherman. He didn't want me to go to the lab that day, but I had gone anyway. Sara, you should have...it was a blood bath. Every human in that place had been murdered by torture and...and worse."

Sara watched as Mel paced. She rubbed her swollen belly and seemed to not realize that she did. Sara placed her hand over her own flat belly and knew that she would be doing the same in a few short months.

"Have you ever found out what happened there, Mel? Why those people were killed? And if Zane was responsible for it all?"

Mel had told her that when she got to the lab she was horrified at the carnage. The dead weren't just killed but torn apart. Sometimes in more than just pieces, but like someone had tossed them against walls and dropped them from incredible heights and they had exploded apart. And she had told her that Zane was injured too, shot in several places, yet she wouldn't tell her what had happened.

"Yes. Just recently. I've been piecing things together for years. Every time I came across one of the...well, I've began to call them inmates, I would just keep adding to the story."

"Inmates? I don't think I like the sound of that. I've heard about what Bailey had to endure. Is it the same?"

Mel sat down and a glass of juice and an apple appeared. She looked up at the ceiling and frowned. Sara just knew it was Shamus. He was a bit overprotective of his mate, it seemed. Mel picked the glass up and twirled it in her hand.

"Oh Sara, it was so much worse. The conditions they were subject to…it makes me shudder to think that they had to live like animals. And the people running it were little more than that themselves. Filth and excrement everywhere and not just what they had done that day either. The cells, little more than boxes with holes that meals, if they got any, were shoved through. I found Zane's and the…she lived like that for decades with nothing more than a towel on the floor and a bucket in the corner for a bathroom. There was a large spray over the entire…they hosed them down twice a month to clean them."

Sara didn't know what to say. She knew from Bailey that she had had a hard time of it, her being a child and growing up like she had. But she'd never said anything close to what Mel was describing. Sara had gotten that the place was clean and well run if one overlooked the fact that they were creating people for their own use.

"So, who did the killings then? You don't think Zane did it, do you? Not anymore, right? So you can release her from her sentence with you now."

"No. No, she didn't. Zane killed the first four men then she passed out from blood loss. She'd been shot several times and had more than likely saved all the people on that floor that day."

Sara could tell there was more, something else besides Sherman being Zane's father. Sara didn't know if she wanted to know. Was positive she didn't.

"If I let her go, release her, she'll want me to release her from everything. Including her life."

CHAPTER 16

Zane had not yet shifted to human from a hawk at the MacManus mansion when she felt a disturbance. Something was…off, she supposed was a good way to describe it. Tasting the air, she knew the scent, but not where it was coming from. It was then that she felt the queen. She was close. Moving just to the door of the house Zane reached to the women in the kitchen and put them on alert.

"Move to the interior of the house. Don't do it quickly, but don't fuck around either. Something comes, but I can't get a…the king needs to stay where he is. He is hidden in the house above you."

Zane felt them both move to the middle of the home. Whatever was tracking them moved as well. Not within the house, but just as Zane was doing outside of it, feeling them move. Only she was aware of it and he wasn't of her.

"Shamus wants to know if he can breach your hold on your mind. He says that he feels it too. He said to let him in through me."

"No. I don't want him in my mind any…keep the vamps close. It knows they move within the house."

"It? What are we dealing with here, Zane? Is it human, vamp, what?"

Zane didn't answer. It was moving again. She took to the air just as he moved away. She spotted him just a mile from the house, slinking along the road in a beat up car. Zane moved lower and

119

tried to get a better scent on the man when she felt Aiden move into her mind.

"Zane? What is it? I can feel that you're in danger. What the hell are you doing now?"

Zane had gone for decades without a single person really bothering her if she didn't count the queen, and now she had a frigging open pathway to everything that she knew. Next thing she'd have the creatures of the earth tapping in for a chat.

"I'm working. If you can't say something constructive then shut the fuck up. Fuck a duck and watch it waddle, you people are a bunch of nosey bee buddies."

"Come back to the bed and I'll help you when—"

"Which bed, Aiden? The one you left me in alone or the one you rested in today? Leave me alone. I've got a job to do."

She closed the connection to him and the rest of the house. Her flight took her just about a mile in front of the car and now she waited for him to pass the branch she was sitting on. It took him less than three minutes to get to where she was. It took her a full minute to realize who she was seeing and another minute before she could wrap her head around it. Taking off again, this time taking her time, Zane headed to the mansion and sat on the roof to think.

If he was in on this then Zane was going to need help. Not just help, but magical help. This man was not supposed to be alive. He'd been killed the day that the others had been; she had done it herself. Phillip. The Phillip from the lab had just driven away from the mansion and was very much alive.

Zane remembered him falling to the floor, his body lying in a pool of blood after she'd taken his hand off that held the gun. She'd left him there knowing, hoping that he would bleed out, that he would die like the others. After she'd passed out the queen had shown up and she never thought to go and check on him and the others. Not that she would have. Now she had to tell the queen what had happened. She had to tell her the truth so that she would know where she had failed. But for now, at this moment, they were all safe. Zane took to the sky once again and went to where the lab had been sitting all those years ago.

There was nothing there really. The grass had all but hidden it from anyone who ventured close. Not that anyone would. The ground was warded against animals moving in and she had purchased the property a very long time ago. The electric fence kept most curious people out and the wolves, wild and hungry, kept out the others. She landed a half mile from the site and then shifted into her panther. It took her less than three minutes to get there.

She walked the perimeter twice and was about to leave it alone and fly over it when she saw the opening. Someone had gone to a great deal of trouble to make sure that she or whomever walked around this area could not see what they had done. The fence had been shorted out and the power had been interrupted here. She got close enough to smell the heat of the power, but not close enough to be hurt by it. This section of wire was not working. Someone had clipped it so that the heavy voltage went around this eight foot section rather than run through it.

Shifting again to human, Zane stood and looked at the damage then around the field. She could see them now, the tire tracks and the other marks as well. She would guess that it was a moving van, something heavy. It also looked as if they had made several trips to this point. Leaning down, she picked up a blade of grass and sniffed.

She didn't know what Simon's scent was, but she did know Phillip's and knew that it would be the same. It had been several decades, but she remembered, remembered as well as if it had happened yesterday. She had to do something about this and do it now before he came back. Moving into the broken area of the fence she moved inside the perimeter of the compound and reached into the ground.

Looking for any sort of living thing beneath the earth proved a little tricky. The creatures that lived below ground took exception to her invasion. Zane apologized to them and moved on. There were a few disturbances that she was able to mend, a bit of black magic here and a little tainted blood there. When she reached the foundation of the old lab, she wasn't surprised to find humans within the walls. She was surprised to find the amount of magic inside. Black mostly, but a bit of white as well.

Zane kept moving within the walls and counted as she went. Twelve humans and sixteen *others,* and there was at least three different species of fae. Against those odds, she couldn't do anything alone but kill everything within, including those seemingly trapped inside. Shifting again, Zane took to the sky and went back to the MacManus household.

~~~

Aiden knew the moment she was within the perimeter of the house. He was making his way up from the lair when he felt her sadness. How profound it was startled him so badly that he had to stop and brace himself against the wall. When he walked into the living room she turned to look at him, but did not stop talking to James.

"...a dozen or so still inside. The place is hot and I think it's working again."

Aaron looked disgusted and Sara looked pale. Mel, the queen, and her mate, Shamus, sat on one of the couches and listened to Zane explain. The only ones who seemed to be talking were her and James.

"Why do you suppose that the lab is...I'm sorry, dear, what did you call it? Hot? I don't believe I know what that means."

"She means it's being run again, as in someone is working it again. How can this be happening again? I thought that they were all destroyed when we left it all those years ago." Bailey had just walked in the room as she spoke.

Aiden watched his brother with Bailey. She looked as if she had been hit and hit hard. When she started pacing in the opposite direction as Zane Aiden had a moment to wonder if all women paced when Zane suddenly stopped in front of him.

He wasn't sure what she was looking at, but he was almost sure it wasn't him. She had a faraway look about her, as if she was thinking hard and using all of her concentration to do so. That's when he felt the fist bit of magic coming from her, a small dose of it first then it grew as she stared at him. He would bet any amount of money that she had no idea she was doing it. He started to reach for her when James cleared his throat.

"Don't. The women of magic do better when they can think on their own. Mel is hard to even get near when she is working out a problem. Let her be, young man, for now at least."

Aiden looked back at James. The man didn't look a day over thirty-five. James grinned, and Aiden knew he'd heard his thoughts. Zane suddenly turned to the queen. Aiden felt her anger as though it were his own.

"I need your permission to tell them. They have a right to know what I am and what I have been to you. I would also ask that you take this connection to Aiden St. James from me and him." Zane pulled away and stood before the queen.

Aiden wasn't sure if he should be terrified for his mate or pissed. He decided to be both. As well as a little insulted.

"I'm not willing to let you go as my mate. And I don't care what you've done in the past or what you may think you've—"

"I'm a fucking killer, you idiot. I killed…those people in that lab died because I wanted to help Eight. And now, now they are back and it's my fault. I didn't check. I didn't go back and check."

"Check what, Zane? The men who actually did this to you and the others? The first men who died that day? I know what happened. I also have a clearer picture in mind why you never told me what really transpired that day. They tortured you, all of you, didn't they? They put you into—"

"You've no fucking idea what we did that day. You've no idea what we had to endure every day. They kept us starved, not only for food and water, but for comfort. Touching and speaking to one another. Did you know that we were fed our one meal on the same tray they cut pieces of us apart on? That there were weeks, sometimes months that would go by and they wouldn't empty out pails that we used to go to the bathroom in. Eight was dying. Was I supposed to let him? Should I have let them drag him—"

"Enough!" Aaron roared with authority. The room grew silent. "We will talk about this calmly and without fault. You'll tell us now, Zane. Tell us now what you think is so horrible that you can't take a mate in Aiden."

Aiden felt her anger and caught himself before he laughed at her. He had been on the receiving end of her wrath once or twice and was happy to see it directed at someone else for a change. But with the looks he was getting now from Zane he knew he wasn't quite off the hook.

"There is something I need to tell you, Zane," Mel started. "Something I should have...I only recently found out about it and it wasn't until just yesterday that I found out its truth. Something, it's about your DNA. I've been...it's—"

"Your mate was my donor? Don't beat yourself up over it. I don't," Zane said.

To say that Mel was shocked would have been a gross understatement on everyone's part. She looked like she'd had the shit scared out of her and then drained as well. Shamus sat her on the couch and then began to rub her back in slow, tight circles. He was grinning like the Cheshire cat.

"How did you...who told you? Him? Did Sherman tell you, or did someone else? And if you knew, why didn't you say anything?"

Zane shrugged. "Didn't see any reason to get my panties in a twist about it. So what? He's the primary donor to my system. And? What does that have to do with the price of eggs in China?"

"Eggs from China? Oh my, Miss Zane, I do believe they have a much better price at the local market. I could order you some if you would like. I do have an order to send out in the morning."

Aiden looked at Duncan who had just walked in with a huge friggin' tray of food and drinks. It seemed every time he saw the man he was passing out food.

"Nah, Duncan, that'll be all right. I don't eat them anyway. But thanks." Zane winked at the man and he blushed. Aiden didn't think he'd ever seen him blush before. Zane turned back to the conversation at hand. "I figured out what he wanted from me right away. I didn't have much say in the matter, not then at any rate. But things soon changed and as I grew stronger he did tend to leave me to the others to deal with."

"But they created you to be some sort of killing machine. He wanted you and others like you for his own army. If you hadn't gotten away he would have destroyed you too." There was pain in Bailey's voice, hurt and terror as well.

"Destroy me? He couldn't destroy me. He would have had to have gotten close and there was no fucking way that was happening. I don't under...you think I was created there? I was created, but not in that lab. I was told I was mixed up in the lab at the castle. And I wasn't one of his experiments. I was one of his donors."

CHAPTER 17

There was a moment when not a sound was made, not even a breath could be heard taken. Aaron looked around the room and realized that they were waiting. Waiting on someone to say something, do something. But Bailey spoke before Aaron could.

"You were a donor. One they used to create what…did you know what he was doing with you? Did you know the type of monsters he was making to work for him? I've lost so much because of…how could you?"

Aaron started to tell Bailey to back off, that it wasn't the way she thought, but he wasn't sure either. But he was prevented from speaking again when Mel did. This time, the pain was in her voice.

"I doubt she had a great deal to say about it, Bailey. Sherman had been…I know about the lab now. It was set up in one of the dungeons deep within the castle. How I missed it for that long is something I'm not proud of. I was so stupid and so naive about him. How could I have…"

"How could you have what? Stopped him? I doubt it. He would have simply set things up elsewhere. Maybe he would have set it up in this world a little sooner. Who knows?" Zane moved to the door. Aaron wondered for a moment if she thought she was leaving. "He's close again. Sinclair, he's within five miles of this place. His heat, his signature is all around us as though he is in flight. You have to know what I…the lab is full of weres, mostly pack animals—wolf, cat. My animal of choice is a panther and I could feel them inside. I didn't know he could…Sinclair has been working with his own DNA. He wants Mrs. MacManus. For a breeder. And the master's realm. He thinks to control the population he needs by becoming the master here."

Aaron nodded. Others had tried, but he had always come out on top. It helped that he wasn't just a vampire, or even a fourteen-hundred-year-old one. But his magic, Sara's magic, made him more. More than anyone bargained for when the challenged him.

"Does he know she is with child? And what is he? I'm assuming he isn't wholly human. What else is he besides a dead man?"

Aaron watched Zane pace a bit more. He respected her for not just assuming. He could feel her frustration at having to involve others in the need to stop this madman. But he also respected her for knowing that she couldn't do this on her own. He glanced over at Aiden. Aaron could almost feel sorry for the man. Almost. But Aaron knew that having a strong and powerful mate had major advantages too.

"No. From what I have seen in his mind, he's slightly off. He seems to think he will rule not only the world, but all creatures within it too. He has no idea what Sara…Mrs. MacManus looks like much less what she is capable of. Most of his knowledge of either of you is from Sherman. And none of that is all that helpful." Her grin told Aaron that it also wasn't very flattering either.

"What is your plan, Zane? I know that you must have one. You have come here for a reason, to meet with us for a purpose. Tell us what you want."

Aaron thought that he knew people well enough. He'd been around them for nearly two millenniums. But Zane didn't act like any other person he'd ever met. She was a force of her own, a being like no other. When she looked at Aiden then at the queen he knew that whatever it was wasn't going to bode well for Aiden and her.

"I want my free—"

"No. I would ask for my boon now. You will bond and mate with me, Zane. I will take my favor that you owe me now."

Aaron was startled by Aiden's sudden demand. As it seemed the others in the room were as well. Mel simply smiled and nodded at him. Zane looked ready to do him bodily harm. Aaron was thankful that as his mate Zane couldn't cause him harm. But that didn't stop her from being royally pissed at him.

"Now? You want this now? No. I refuse. You had your chance and you didn't take...I have plans of my own, you moronic jackass. I won't bond with you unless she says it's not permanent. I won't...why? Damn it!"

"I will and I do. Now. If you will all excuse us, Zane and I have some unfinished business to attend to. Zane?"

Aaron was sure that Aiden was counting on her not being able to harm him or he would have taken precautions. When Zane moved toward the door Aiden followed, but at a safe distance. It was all Aaron could do not to burst out laughing when she suddenly stopped and Aiden took a hasty step or two back. Staring at Aiden, Zane spoke.

"What happens to him if he bonds with me? Does he only live if I do? And if so, is that a part of your grand plan to make me suffer more? If so then I will fight this until you give in. I won't be a part of his death."

Mel spoke, her voice hard and unforgiving. "He becomes all that you are. And yes, without you he dies. Without you, Aiden St. James will starve and die. But as for being a part of this...if you mean do I want you to be safe and alive, then yes. Do you mean did I make him your mate? Then no. That is the Sisters Three, not me. That was our bargain when I created them." Mel stood, went to Aiden, and stood before him. "You leave or you refuse him, then he dies. You let him become your mate, your bonded mate, then the two of you will be more powerful than you've ever imagined, anyone would have ever imagined."

"I don't want this. Haven't I told you this before? I want to die. I want to quit. Please, you promised me that if I told you...they came for Eight. They were going to use him for another donor. Do you know how they did that? They would stimulate him until he ejaculated. Then they would take his sperm and his blood and create little babies from that part of him. It was so clinically done that we didn't even think of it as sex, or even relief. It was rape. My eggs were removed from me every…I have no idea how many babies were…she's mine." Aaron was stunned when she pointed at Bailey. "I can feel the connection. That's what he did. Sinclair or Phillip would take and make beings that had no idea why or what they were being created for. Please, I've had enough, let me go."

Aiden walked to her and picked her up. When Zane started to struggle against him he simply tossed her over his shoulder and strode from the room. Aaron looked around the room and then laughed. If the situation wasn't so grim he might have thought it was the funniest thing he'd ever seen.

Aiden was angry. No, that wasn't true, he was pissed off. She was not going to get away from him and she had forced his hand. Something he didn't want, nor did he like that he'd had to do. He slammed the door shut behind them when he got to his lair.

"Are you going to behave when I put you down? I want to talk to you. For now anyway."

"If you're asking me if I plan to hurt you then not only yes, but fuck yes. I'm going to rip you apart. I'm going to shift into something big and eat you alive. Put me the—you fucking hit my ass again and I will tear your—damn it, Aiden, I'm going to hurt you."

The third swat to her ass made him smile. If she kept this up, he'd be as hard as stone before she ever touched the bed. As it was his cock ached badly, as did his fangs. Need was riding him hard and the knowledge that Zane was about to be his made his beast ride beneath his skin.

"You'll do well to hush and listen to me. You know that you accepted my boon and I'm going to collect. Now. Tonight. We are going to become one, Zane, willingly."

"I don't want you. You can just fuck off. Put me down. I can't breathe this way. I mean it."

"If you can talk, you can certainly breathe. Now here is what's going to happen. I'm going to strip you down to that delicious bare skin of yours then I'm going to start at your feet and work my way up your body until I get to your pussy. Once there I'm going to—"

"If you think for one second that I'm going to have sex with you then you're crazier than I first thought." This smack was loud and he could feel the burn in his hand. "You hit me again, you bastard, and I'll remove your dick so fast that you'll piss sitting down for the rest of your life. Which may not be much longer."

Aiden brought her down off his shoulder and level with his body, but held her close. He'd learned over the years that weres couldn't shift if they were held too close to another being. And the way that he was holding Zane, there was no way she could do it without hurting him. But that didn't stop her from trying.

Aiden reached up to her backside again and felt her tense. Instead of hitting her butt again he grabbed the waist of her pants and ripped them from her. Her silence was deafening. Aiden ran his hand up the curve of her ass and then down again. He could smell her response. It was hot and immediate.

"I'm going to enjoy this, taking you. I have looked forward to it for a very long time. To drinking from you, making love to you, with you. I want to make you mine, Zane."

"Don't do this, Aiden. I'm not a…please stop that. I can't think when you…oh, Aiden."

Her body shifted around his waist as he entered the long crack of her ass with just the tip of his finger. Her moan went straight to his cock and made him need to reach down and adjust himself before he caused serious damage to his cock. But he didn't. He wanted to get her nearly screaming with need before he stopped.

"You're getting wet, love. I can smell it. Your heat and need are making your scent strong and irresistible to me." He deepened his finger, gathering her cream and moving up to her tight bud. "Hummm, this is where I want to be. Deep in you here, my cock moving in and out of your tightness."

Aiden decided that now would probably be a good time to move to something they could lie down on, something with a lot of room. He stood next to the bed, but continued his torment of her body. As he gathered more of her juices on his fingers, he pressed his little finger against her bundle of nerves and entered her. She nearly tossed them both to the floor with her jerk against him.

"Aiden, please. I don't...I need you there too. Please. Fuck me. Now, please fuck me hard."

"Make us naked, Zane. I want to feel you against my skin. Take our clothes now."

He was naked. Just like that, his cock was rigid and straining from his groin. His body hot and hard for hers, his fangs dropped and hungry. Slowly moving his palm along her thigh and up the curve of her Aiden savored the feel of her skin, the warm silkiness of her.

"Aiden, please, I hurt with need. Let me down to touch you, to feel you." Zane was practically crawling up onto his shoulder she had leaned up so high. It was all he could do to keep her there, to hold her for his exploration. Slowly, he moved her down his waist, bringing her breasts to his mouth before he let her go any further.

Hungrily he fed at them, her nipples first then her whole breast. They tasted ripe and full, her nipples pebbled in his mouth. Aiden scraped his fangs over them and wanted to bite her, to taste her there, feed from her. When she wrapped her legs around his waist tighter, it freed his hands to cup the heavy flesh and bring them both to his mouth to suckle. Her pussy curved around the tip of his cock, wetting them both with her juices. Her small moans and growls were doing things to him he'd never felt before. His blood stirred, heated his body to the point of near pain for her.

With her legs around him Aiden lowered them to the bed. He wanted more than anything to turn her to her belly and plunder that sweet ass of hers, but the need to be deep inside of her wet, hot pussy was driving him to the brink. Her scent, strong with her own need, was making him as close to the edge as he'd ever been in his life.

"Bite me...Christ, I'm so close to spilling my seed on you. Feed from me over my heart, Zane. I'll...I will feed from you when we come. I want to mark you, make you mine, but if we don't hurry, we'll—Zane, baby, don't do that, not yet."

She was suckling at his nipple, her teeth—her fangs, he could feel now—were just to the point of breaking skin, almost but painfully not yet. Aiden could feel his heart pounding as he reached for the dagger. The dagger of his family, the one that would make them one.

Aiden was of royal blood, as was his brother Tristan, and he too had used this same blade to bond him to Bailey. With this there was a ceremony where they used a family heirloom, a jeweled dagger, and cut a vein over their hearts to drink from there. This exchange was more of a ritual than a need, but it was still practiced today, especially by the pure-blooded vampires.

With dagger in hand Aiden sat up and looked down at her. Zane was his mate, his life, and he wanted her consent, not this forced way of taking her. He would take her anyway, but he wanted her to say she wanted him as well.

"Zane, I need you to want this as well. I want you to tell me that you will willingly take me as your mate, please. I don't want this to color our future together."

She stared at him for a long moment and then she sat up on her elbows. Her need was still in her eyes, her body, but she was looking less needy and more pissed as the seconds ticked by.

"And if I don't, what will you do? Take me anyway? Make me something to you that we both know could or will get one or both of us dead? This isn't right, Aiden. I'm not Suzy Homemaker and I don't do tea parties. I can't be whatever you think I might be for you. I'm a killer, not a vampire, not a were. I'm a killer."

Aiden took the knife in his fist and sliced it across his chest just over his heart. He felt the pain of it. His blood began to flow from the wound, but he didn't try and stop it. He leaned down, dropping the knife on the floor beside the bed and looked her in the eyes. "I want you to drink from me because you want to. I want you to be my mate because you need me as much as I need you, love me as much as I love you. If you don't, if you'd rather leave me now, then do it. I'd rather bleed out than to force you into something that I know we will both regret."

Aiden rolled to his back and threw his arm over his eyes. If she left him now he would die. He wasn't being dramatic, he was being honest. Honest with her as much as he was himself. He couldn't do it, couldn't make her be his mate, not if it would cost her trust.

He felt her move off the bed and then back onto it. He moved his arm from his face when she pulled it back. He looked up at her as she moved over his body, her thighs on either side if his hips. She took his hands in hers and settled them on her hips.

"I do want you, but you must know that if you do this you become me and my magic. All of it, including the tats. They are a part of me as much as anything else."

"I don't ink. Vamps, they can't ink. We heal too fast. But whatever else you want, I will gladly take from you. Anything. I love you."

"You don't get it. I'm not asking you to become like me, Aiden. You will become like me, tats too. They are in my makeup, a part of me. That's why I can have them. You'll have them as well if you want this."

Sitting up, her body poised over his, Aiden ran his hands over the weapons on her hips then higher over her ribs. They were warm, almost hot to his touch. Once he reached her neck, he could feel the ones at the back of her neck and then the one along her spine. Was what she said true? Would he wear them as she did? He didn't know. He actually didn't care either. Whatever she was, whatever she had, he'd willingly learn to live with it to have her.

"Take me into you, Allison. I want you to be with me, all of you. I will have to learn to do what you do, but I want you to take me into you."

Zane leaned forward and licked the blood still seeping from the cut over his left nipple. His breath caught when she got to the wound and she hesitated. Looking up at him again, she closed her mouth over it and drew him in. Aiden lifted her slightly and lowered her over his cock slowly. She was wet, hot and tight. It was everything he could do not to throw back his head and howl.

Rolling her to her back he began moving in her, deep, long strokes as she feed from him. When he could feel his own climax nearly upon him he lifted her wrist to his mouth and licked the pounding pulse there.

"Come, Allison. Come now and be mine."

As soon as her body, her sheath, tightened around his cock he bit into her wrist. Her response was immediate and so was his. He drank from her even as he filled her with his seed, marking them both as a couple, marking them as a pair.

Aiden sealed the wound at her wrist as she licked the cut closed at his heart. He couldn't move just yet, but savored the feel of her sated body over his. He closed his eyes even as he shifted off her and pulled her body close.

"You won't regret this, Allison. I swear to you that I will do everything in my power to keep you happy."

She snuggled under his chin as she answered. "I hope you don't, Aiden. And don't call me Allison."

CHAPTER 18

Zane moved along the halls toward the upper floors quietly. She wasn't leaving the house; she just needed to breath for a moment. And to get away from the man she had just bonded her life to. She may have turned the other way if she had been paying more attention to her surroundings, but being so deep in thought she was upon the occupants of the kitchen before she knew it. And turning back was taken from her the moment the woman spoke.

"I don't think so. Come back here now. I think we have a few things to discuss you and me, don't you?"

"Not that I can think of. I want to get some air. And talking to you won't help my disposition one bit." Zane didn't move, but then neither did the queen.

"Sit down, Zane. I know that you've bonded and mated with Ai—"

"Not any of your concern. Say your piece and then leave me alone. Our deal was you stay out of my personal life. Not pretend that you give a shit."

Zane knew she'd pissed Mel off again; her anger was hot and Zane could almost taste it. But she knew long ago that no matter what she did, the queen never hurt her, not physically anyway.

"All right. But could you at least sit down? I'm tired and I'm achy, also not really anything you care about, but I just...please, Allison, sit down and talk to me. I need to know what you know about my...about Sherman."

Zane started to give her a flippant answer, but could see the hurt in Mel's eyes. She knew what Sherman had done to her; hell, there were few people in the magical kingdom who didn't. But right now Mel looked...defeated.

"I hated the prick. He was a sadist bastard that played with people and their lives like it was his right. Someone should have castrated him at birth."

Mel burst out laughing. "Why don't you just tell me like it is, Zane? No sense in beating around the bush."

Zane moved to the kitchen door and opened it. She waited for the queen to say something about it, but Zane simply stood in the open doorway and looked out. She needed to get this over with and they both knew it.

"When I killed James, he'd shot me. Several times, as a matter of fact. I was losing blood quickly and I had been so weak that it was all I could do to get back into my cell and close the door. Hell had broken loose in the sublevels and nothing was safe from the others. I didn't...I tried to regain control, but without feeding on one of them I couldn't do it."

"How many were in that lab? I'd heard different amounts, but none of them were very accurate, I think. Anywhere from fifty to a hundred is what I'd heard."

Zane looked up when Sara entered the room, Aaron beside her. Before she could answer the queen Aiden came in as well. Zane didn't move from the doorway, but did shift to lean against the jamb.

"Counting the ones on my level there were almost nine hundred of us. Fifty-two of us were donors, the rest were other breeders. There were about three hundred women, fertile, and some two hundred that were trying to carry the spawns the lab boys made. They were having minimal success."

Zane grinned at Aaron's observation. "You were keeping them from succeeding, weren't you? How? Were you doing something to the test or just using magic?"

"Magic. Mostly anyway. There were a few of us strong enough that when we worked together we could make the tests get too hot and kill off the samples in the lab. It was that or have to put up with knowing that they were making whatever it was they were working toward. I think Sherman knew, that's why he had us put in the lowest levels of the lab. I don't think he counted on that having the opposite effect. Being under the labs simply made it easier to use the vents upward to collect their energy and pull it into us."

Aiden didn't move. She didn't have to look at him to feel his anger. She wanted to tell him "I told you so," but kept looking into the night. It was a safer feeling for some reason.

"They came down—the lab boys came down to my level about once a month. They couldn't be there much more than that. We were all very strong and without Sherman they couldn't control us and our combined strength. There were ten of us. The first two cells held a pair of wolves who they thought could breed. We all knew that without them being mates, that nothing would ever become of it, but hey, they had fun. Cell three was a fae, though I'm not sure what flavor she was."

"Flavor? You mean type of fae? And did you know anyone's name, their surnames?" Sara asked as she moved around the kitchen getting drinks for everyone.

"Yeah and no. I meant type of and no on the surnames. We, none of us, had any that I'm aware of. I had been there first; I wasn't created there, but at the castle. The one you live at." She pointed in the general direction of Mel. "I don't remember much of that one, but the one I...the one that I finally left I remember very well. Four through seven held vampires that I know weren't very old, maybe less than a couple hundred years. Eight and ten were both succubae, eight a sex succubus and ten, anger. I'm not sure what they thought keeping those two together could do, but they tried to make them breeders as well. As with most paranormal, without them being mated they couldn't reproduce either. I was...I guess I was them all. I could do what they did and then some. But mostly I made their lives as much a living hell as I could."

"How long were you there, Zane? I'm assuming it was awhile. About how long?"

Zane looked at Aiden. She knew they all thought she was much younger than she really was. No one had ever cared much before now so she didn't feel the need to share. She glanced at Mel and at her nod she looked out the door again. "I'm...I'm nearly four thousand years old. Sherman created me when he had first mated Mel. Her mother was still the reigning queen."

Zane waited. She knew that it was quite the bombshell and wanted more than anything to turn and see what they were doing, but she simply stood where she was. It was hard not to just shift and leave. She was surprised when she heard Aiden speak her name.

"Allison, come here. I want to hold you, please." His voice was soft, almost too soft for anyone to hear, but she didn't turn and look, just closed her eyes and continued.

"He told me that I was going to be the future. That I was going to be his best creation yet. There were others, more than...fifty-three of them, but they died after the first few months after we left the castle. He thought it was the loss of magic that is characteristically a part of the realm, but that wasn't it. It was the air. The...it wasn't pure."

"Then how did you...I'm sorry, that sounds crass. But how did you manage to survive when the others hadn't?"

Zane looked at the queen again then out the door. It was easier to speak like this. "They were dying. All of them. I couldn't save them, I tried, but I couldn't save them."

"So you took their essences. You had to survive, Zane. You did nothing wrong when you took what they didn't need any longer. You had to survive."

Zane turned in the jamb and looked at Aaron. She knew that, of anyone at the table, he would understand what she had done, but she wasn't mated to him. She didn't look at Aiden when she continued, but at Aaron. "As I grew stronger I also grew to hate what I was. I couldn't die, I knew that in the back of my mind somehow, but I could hate. It was all I had to begin with. Then once the hate began to eat me alive I started to...to act out on it. The years I was in this realm were...I killed so much, so many. I wanted someone, anyone to hurt me, to hunt me down. But that grew to be too little too. After a while I began to turn my energies into helping those around me until I saved Liberty. She was a witch." Taking a deep breath she moved into the kitchen and began to remove Aiden's shirt she had on. It covered the sleeveless t-shirt under it and hid her marks too.

"I had this book, one that I had stolen from the kingdom. It was called *Nam eget Art* or *Living Body Art.* I would put the weapons on my body and she made them a part of me, my DNA. According to that book, it would be passed on to anyone who I became a part of." Zane heard Aiden shift. "As it turned out, it worked. As the weapons became more advanced, I put them to me as well."

She pulled the shirt off and lifted the tee side where the blade was. It was beautiful if one looked past how deadly it looked on her skin. Turning around, Zane lifted her shirt up and showed them the one on her back. Aiden was suddenly in front of her, shielding her front from view. When she looked up at him, he smiled and kissed her on the nose. To say she was shocked would have been an understatement.

"Christ. They're…well hell, Zane, they're beautiful. And they work how? I'm assuming you can use them with the name *living* associated with them." She glanced back at Aaron and nodded.

Reaching behind her, she wrapped her hand around the handle and peeled it away from her skin, leaving the scabbard in place. She turned as Aiden lowered her shirt and handed it pommel first to Aaron. He didn't hesitate, but took it from her hand with a short nod. When he had tested its weight in his hand for several seconds, he suddenly looked at Aiden. *Now,* she thought, *now comes the truth.*

"You have mated and bonded with her, correct?"

Zane felt Aiden come up behind her and hold her. She assumed he answered his master. Aiden's arm slipped around her waist and he pulled her back to his chest.

"Good." Zane stared at the master as he continued. "This is very good. Now, if there is nothing more you feel the need to share, I believe we have a being to take care of. What are your plans and how do we help?"

"Wait. What? You know that he'll be like me? He'll have these same...why are you nodding like that? I've made him...he's not just a vamp anymore, but a creature like me. Doesn't that bother you?"

"First of all, you are not a creature. You're a passionate woman." Aaron turned toward Mel when she snorted and frowned. "As I was saying," he continued to Zane, "a passionate woman who is mated to a vampire in my realm. Secondly, very little 'bothers' me when someone is happy that I care about. I would like to learn more about you and this book, but for now, we have other more pressing needs to contend with. Now, let's get this party started."

~~~

P. Simon Sinclair sat in his office and stared at the man in front of him. He couldn't have heard him correctly. There was just no way that what he said could be even remotely true.

"You say what again? And this time, you'd better have a different story than the bullshit you just handed me. Start from the top."

The man swallowed hard. Simon couldn't remember his name, not that he would have even if he'd told him right now. This man, this person, wasn't important enough to have Simon remember. People like this man were here to serve Simon and he'd better, by God, start remembering that.

"I said, sir, that Mr. MacManus is asking for an interview with you. He said that it is concerning his wife. And he told me to tell you that he won't take no for an answer."

Simon looked at the clock on his desk. It was just after ten in the morning. This man, MacManus, was reputed to be a vampire, a very stupid one at that. Maybe his information was wrong. He stiffened at that. Sherman had always told him if you want it done correctly, then do it your fucking self. Simon caught the grin before it did more than make his face look like it was snarling.

"Tell Mr. MacManus that I'm a very busy man and that I don't have the time today. If he'd like to come back tomorrow then—"

Simon's door slammed open and against the wall beside it. Power preceded the man and woman who entered, more than Simon had ever felt before. His cock actually stirred with it. Simon started to rise and was stopped by invisible bands around his waist and his wrists holding him to the chair.

"I have time now, Sinclair, and you'll do well to see me. I'm Aaron Xavier MacManus, Master Vampire of this realm. I would have a word with you."

"You can't just barge in here. This is my office. I will have security remove you from here this instant." And just that quickly Simon was lifted up off the floor, chair and all.

"Cease. You'll shut up and listen to me or, so help me, I will drain you where you sit. As I was saying, I'm Aaron Xavier MacManus and—"

"Darling," the woman standing next to the large vamp said. "Do get on with it. I'm supposed to meet Mel for lunch in an hour and if you start over every time this idiot says anything we could be here until you need to feed again. And unless Sinclair here wants to be your meal, then I'm afraid you will be a very, very hungry vampire."

Simon started to say something more, but the woman looked at him. There was something very…terrifying in her eyes. Almost as if she wanted him to interrupt again just to see if the vamp would drain him. MacManus kissed the beautiful woman and turned back to Simon. The vamp had changed. Drastically. His fangs were showing and not only that, but his eyes had turned a blood red as well. And Simon was sure that the man had actually grown taller as well as wider, looming over Simon as if he was a child in a child's chair. As he advanced Simon felt fear, the kind of fear that had one wetting his or her pants and wondering if a person would see the morning. Backing away in the chair he started to—*beep beep beep beep.*

Simon shot up in bed immediately. His heart was pounding and he was covered in sweat. The room, pitch black in the night,

143

now had shadows and sounds he'd never heard before. He lay back down and continued to stare hard around his bedroom, just knowing that somewhere the big vamp was hiding.

Simon had been having a lot of nightmares lately. Most of them had to do with his friend Sherman and their times together, but then the man who he had just dreamed about had come to him as well. Unlike the dreams with Sherman, Simon never remembered what the man looked like or the woman with him. She never said the same thing twice, but it was always quite clear that without her, Simon would be dead.

Knowing that he wasn't going to get any more sleep tonight Simon got up and went into the bathroom to shower. Turning on the water and stripping down as best he could with one hand, he stood and looked at himself in the mirror that was steaming up as he stood there.

He wasn't as muscled as he'd once been. It was the magic, he knew. Black magic had a way of draining a person and as much as Simon used it to get what he wanted, it was small wonder that he was a little on the thin side. His hair, once his pride, was now stringy and lank on his head. Moving his fingers through the patches his fingers came away with several more strands of it. His teeth were beginning to show wear as well. He wasn't so sure that he liked the after effects of his magic, but the power it gave him was well worth it.

As he stepped under the spray Simon wondered when Sherman was coming back. It had been years since he'd seen him. Simon wasn't too worried. Sherman had often told him that he had other business to attend to and that Simon shouldn't be too concerned if he didn't come around for a while. But it had been about ten years now...no, more like fifteen. And the money, Sherman should come back to give Simon more money at least. There had been none for a very long time. But the lab was coming along.

They had set up the lab a few months before Sherman disappeared. He told Simon that he had a new breeder and a donor that he wanted to acquire for them. They were both females. Simon didn't like dealing with the donors. They were usually too strong for him and the limited amount of magic Sherman had bestowed on him. Now there were several donors and a few breeders residing in the lab awaiting results. Simon laughed when he thought about how clever they'd been about using the old lab to begin again. Sherman had said it was the perfect hiding place.

"Nothing like hiding out in the open, Simon dear. No one would think twice about us coming back here to continue on. I'm betting that bitch Mel wouldn't even give this place a second thought when she comes looking for me."

Sherman had been right. No one had come around since they'd opened up again and the fencing kept anybody from just wandering upon the doorway to the sublevels. Simon shut off the water as he thought about the small twinge he'd gotten yesterday. Something...he wasn't sure what it was, but it gave him the willies. Driving to the lot to be picked up by security, Simon tried to remember the couple and why the name MacManus seemed so familiar.

145

CHAPTER 19

Zane knew the moment that Aiden walked up behind her. She'd come outside for a little fresh air, which she just couldn't seem to get enough of lately. He didn't say anything for long moments, but she felt her peace interrupted all the same. She knew they had a lot to talk about, but she just wanted...no, she needed it to be quiet.

"I can feel your frustration with me. I'm sorry. I just wanted to make sure you were all right. And to ask you about the tats."

"What about them?" She wasn't going to deny her frustration. What would be the point?

"I don't know how to use them. I mean...they appeared just after rising tonight and I don't have a clue what the fuck I'm suppose to do with them. In actuality, they scare the shit out of me."

Zane turned to him. She was surprised by his admission. She'd expected him to want to show her how to use them or even to tell her that she couldn't until he let her. She stood up and walked toward him. "You'll need to touch them, all of them to let them...I don't know, get to know you, I guess. They can't be taken from you unless you allow it. Here, take off your shirt and I'll show you."

Her breath caught when he pulled the shirt he had on over his head. She'd had sex with his man several times, but this was the first time she'd actually gotten a good look at him. She was very glad for the full moon.

"You keep looking at me like that, Allison, and the lesson won't get very far."

Zane looked up into his eyes, searching for his reason for saying something like that to her. All she could see was need and something else she'd never seen before in a person's face. She shook her head. She was being fanciful because she was sure it looked like he needed her for more than sex.

"You're left handed so reach up and put your hand around the pommel of the blade at your back, like this." She turned around and showed him how to do it without removing her own shirt.

"Show me. Take off your shirt and show me. No one will see us and if someone did come up, it's not like we wouldn't know it long before they found us."

He was right. She pulled the t-shirt over her head and left on her bra. She didn't usually wear one like this, but after they'd had sex she wanted something pretty against her skin. She could have made herself anything she wanted, and was slightly embarrassed that she'd chosen this one. She flushed when he drew in a sharp breath and she started to pull her shirt back on.

"Don't. I…Christ, you are the most beautiful woman I've ever seen. Show me this before I forget what we're doing and I take you right here on the ground or against that tree."

Her body responded to his words immediately and Aiden growled low in his throat. She didn't know what he'd meant to do with that growl, but all it did to her was heat her up more. Turning around so that she could show him how to pull his blade, she tried to get a handle on her body.

"Reach behind you and you'll feel the heat of the weapon before you touch it. It will almost feel as if it moves into your hand. Feel it?"

"Yes." She smiled at the excited tone in his voice. "Will it be painful when I pull it away?"

"No. It won't feel like anything. Just pull it out in a long pull or it will return to the scabbard."

Zane turned and watched him pull it from his back. He pulled it as though he'd done it before. That's when she realized that at his age, he probably had. When he came around to face her with the blade in his hand she saw that the mark had adjusted to fit him and his body mass. She waited until he was comfortable with the weight then she moved in with her blade drawn.

"They won't fight one another if we are of the same mindset. See." She tried several times to show him how they repelled each other and wouldn't even come together. "Now think about learning to fight with it and me showing you."

When he nodded, she hit his blade hard enough to make it sing. He grinned like a kid with his first toy.

They moved along the forest floor for several moves before they started to get used to each other. Zane was impressed with Aiden's ability. She would have thought he'd be a novice, but was glad to see that not only was he very competent, but he seemed to listen to her when she told him what to do. And after only an hour he seemed to know what to do and how his body would move with the blade. He returned it to his back before she could warn him. He was on the ground in seconds.

"You have to feed it before you return it. I'm sorry. You were too quick for me."

He glared up at her from his position on the ground. "Feed it? And just so you know, I can hear your laughter about this and don't think for one second I won't make you pay. Tell me how to feed my blade."

She gave him her arm and he pulled his body up with hers. He looked down at her from his imposing height and then kissed her on the mouth. It was quick, but no less scorching. Zane stared at him until he said her name.

"Feed it. Right. It is a part of you so it will require nourishment as well. Blood. Yours now, but in battle or fights, it will feed from your enemy. The more you fight with it, the more it will require. But it will continue to feed as long as you need it."

She thought for sure he was going to balk at it, but he just nodded at her. She sliced the blade along her forearm and then laid the flat of the blade in the blood. They watched as the blade, dull from their play, brightened and gleamed as it took her blood across its design.

Aiden did the same. He looked up at her as his blade fed. "I have two guns on my hips; please tell me that I don't have to shoot myself to feed them."

Zane laughed. She couldn't help herself. He'd been so serious that she couldn't hold it in. "No. Not shoot. The guns feed differently because you don't keep the bullets. They require you to feed them before you load your gun. Same with the extra clips. Just open a little slice and let them touch it."

She showed him how to use the other armament on his body along with how to put them away when finished. He'd been very serious with her and listened to her every word. When it was nearing dawn, he walked her back to the mansion.

"I'm not used to a mate any more than you are, Zane. I think we have a lot to learn about each other. But when you're sad or frustrated with me, it's in my blood to make you better or happy. Give me time is all I ask."

"I don't know a lot about being around people. I work for Danny and before him, others like him. People that leave me alone and don't ask questions. Danny is the longest I've stayed in one spot. I love him and Russell."

Aiden nodded. She could feel his own frustration at her liking another male, but she wasn't giving up their friendship just because he got his panties in a twist over them. He stopped suddenly and she tensed for whatever he had felt. But his mouth covering hers prevented her from asking what.

As he walked her backwards she started to stumble. He simply lifted her up his body by cupping her ass and brought her mound over his hard cock as he kept walking. When she felt the tree rub against her back she arched into his body.

"Watching you swing that blade, it was everything I could do not to toss you to the ground and fuck you. Christ, woman, the things you do to me. Make us naked, Allison. I want to feel your body touching mine."

She started to do it then stopped and pulled his head up so that she could look into his eyes. "You do it. You have every ability that I do. Will them away. This is…oh yes, Aiden, that's perfect."

His body was hot and hard and she could feel his cock nudging her ass cheeks even as he suckled at her breast. His fangs scraping across her nipples made her want him to bite her there, suckle for real as he fed from her. Before she could beg him to take her he growled low in his throat, dropped her down, and stepped back.

"Lean back against the tree and spread your legs. I'm going to lick that pussy of yours until I get my fill, then I'm going to fuck you until neither of us can stand."

Aiden reached to his ankle, pulled the smaller of the two knives there free, and stabbed it into the tree behind her. "Hold your hands around that. If you let go I'll quit and fuck your ass hard. Stay there until I've had my fill and I'll fuck you in your ass hard." He grinned. She reached up and wrapped her hands around the handle of his blade.

"You'll have to feed your knife before you put it back." Zane almost didn't recognize her voice; it was hard and husky.

"Not until I have my fill." He dropped to the ground in front of her and looked up at her as he ran his fingers along her knee to her thigh. "I'm going to fuck you with my mouth and then when you come, I'm going to bite you here."

Zane moaned and nodded to him. She wanted that more than she wanted her next breath. Slowly he leaned his head toward her and she could already feel her juices start to trickle down her thighs. Using his hands he spread her nether lips open and worried her clit with his tongue, not touching anything else.

"Please, Aiden. I need your mouth to take me. Please, now."

He wouldn't be rushed apparently and no matter how much she tried to get him to move into her he continued to play with her nubbin. When she felt his fingers just at her entrance she nearly let go of the blade to guide him where she wanted him, but his slight hesitation made her remember what he'd promised. When he moved lower, pressing his finger just inside of her, she wanted to scream at him to finish, but knew that would only make him go slower.

When he lifted her leg up and settled it over his shoulder Zane was beyond thought. Her body was aching with unfulfilled need. When his finger moved inside of her she rode it with abandonment and need. When she felt him stretch her, moving more fingers in, she started begging him to let her come. The closer she got to paradise the more he backed off a little more. She was going to take her knife from her back and remove his fucking head if he kept it up. When she was ready to do just that he plunged his finger into her ass as he took her with his tongue. She came with a scream.

Over and over he fucked her pussy with his tongue and her ass with his finger. Climax after climax ripped through her until she was no longer holding the blade at her head to keep from touching him, but merely to hang on and keep upright. Her body couldn't take much more and he didn't seem to care. Until, panting, Aiden stood up, his cock a mouthwatering display of male. She wanted to take him as he'd done her, but he growled at her to get on the ground on her knees.

Dropping down, she was just getting up on her knees when she felt him behind her. He wrapped his arm around her waist and pulled her back to him and straight onto his cock, impaling her onto him. She screamed out his name as another powerful climax ran over her.

Aiden leaned down and covered her body with his, pressing her head to the ground and his hips over hers. When he grabbed a handful of her hair and pulled her head back she felt the pain/pleasure of his need all the way to her core. His cock thickened inside of her until she was sure he was going to hurt her, but he bit her shoulder and nothing else mattered.

He slammed into her, hard, quick jabs until she was sure he was going to be raw from it. Over and over Aiden fucked her. When he pulled her back as he sat up on his heels she felt his cock press against her womb tight, almost painfully so. He moved her hair then, her blood trickling down her shoulder from his bite, and he licked her pulse at her throat. When she felt his fingers pinch her clit she came again, screaming his name until she was hoarse, his own cries of completion mingling with hers.

They sat that way for several minutes. Each of them breathing hard with sweat pouring off them. She knew he had to be hurting, his ankles screaming in pain, but he pulled her back when she started to move off him.

"Don't, baby. I just need to hold you for a minute longer."

She stayed until she had to move or fall asleep over him.

At minutes before the dawn they were in the bath in his room, Aiden holding her as she washed her legs. Neither of them said anything, not about the sex in the woods nor the new tats he had on his body. They talked about mundane things. Aiden about his family and Zane about her odd jobs.

"I have to go to Danny's in a little while. I have to put an engine in an SUV. The idiot didn't maintain it so it seized up. I promised Danny I'd do it."

She thought he was going to try and tell her she couldn't go, but he surprised her again. "How long will it take you? I could...I could come and get in your way for you."

Zane laughed. It was becoming less harsh sounding the more she did it. She was also getting less and less startled by it when it burst from her mouth. She lifted her leg and rubbed the sponge along it. Aiden's growl made her feel something stir again.

"It'll take a couple of days. I've already got the old one out, but the new one will have to be lifted up while I put all the parts back on it where they belong. Then I have to do the timing chain and belts. I'm sure you would be a professional at getting in my way, but I really need to concentrate on what I'm doing and you'd be a distraction."

He didn't say anything more until they were getting out of the tub and he was drying her off. "I want to tell you to stay here." Zane started to object, but his raised hand stopped her. "But I know that you are more than likely better equipped and trained at taking care of yourself than I am. I hate that, but it's the truth. Could you at least promise me that you'll try to stay safe until I can leave to come to you?"

Again, he surprised her. She almost said that she'd stay here with him, but she'd made a promise and couldn't break it even if she wanted to. It was the queen's rule and she was stuck with it.

"I'll give it my best shot, but I can't make any promises." He kissed her, then lifted her up and took her to bed. She was beginning to enjoy snuggling. She'd never been much of a "snuggle" type of girl, but with Aiden she could get used to the idea.

CHAPTER 20

"Run it again. I don't care what you think it will do to it, run the fucking test again."

Simon watched as the lab attendant drew more blood from the breeder. It whimpered, but it no longer struggled like it had before. Of course, they'd cut it up pretty badly taking samples from it.

Simon never thought of the breeders as anything but 'its.' To him, they weren't even human much less something he thought should have feelings, same with the donors. They were simply a means to an end and he meant to get as much out of it before he had to either kill it or burn its carcass to get rid of it.

When the vial was full, they both stepped over to the microscope and Simon watched as the lab boy put a small drop on a strip of glass. Why they had to draw so much blood for so little amount was beyond him, but then it wasn't as if they didn't have a near endless supply of the breeders. All he had to do to get more was go to the street corner, flash a twenty, and viola! More test bunnies. He nearly giggled at his own joke, but knew that this man, Dr...Dr. something wouldn't get it. No one had the same sense of humor he did—the idiots.

The guy was shaking now. Good, keep them on their toes, Sherman had told him. A scared employee was much better than one that respected you, and a terrified one would get you the results that you wanted. Simon stepped away to pull out his little notebook.

He was going to write a book someday soon. It was going to be a Golden Globe winner for sure, he thought. He and Sherman were going to co-write it. He already had a title picked out: *Cutting Out the Fat*. Simon thought it was perfect and the little double meaning would be lost on all but the few whom where as brilliant as he and Sherman.

Simon thought again about this mentor. Where was he? And his money? They were getting into serious issues here. The lab boys were demanding paychecks that didn't bounce and Simon needed to make a payment on the new computer. It was going to help him write the next greatest novel of all times. The lab boys weren't too much of a problem; he just fed them to the donors when they got too demanding. Simon looked over at the idiot at the microscope. Maybe he'd be fodder next.

"It's the same, sir. She's not pregnant. And from these tests and the others, she won't breed either."

Simon cuffed him across the mouth. "I told you they are its or whatever their cell numbers are. I don't want to know what their sex is, understand?"

"Yes, sir, but only women can breed. I just thought—" His scream rent the air.

Simon didn't even realize that he'd picked up the scalpel until it was sticking out of the lab boy's eye. Blood was squirting everywhere and the thing on the table tried to get away, it screamed and screamed. Simon snapped. He jerked it from the table and snapped its neck. Its screams were cut off abruptly.

Simon basked in the silence for several seconds as he closed his eyes and stood over the dead woman. When the lab boy whimpered Simon opened one eye, glared at him, and he shut up. It was suddenly all too much. This was all that woman's fault. If she hadn't taken his hand he'd be a great scientist now and not have to depend on the idiots he had now. He remembered that day as though it were yesterday.

They had all gone to the sublevels to get that one called Eight. It was time for him to pony up and give them the sample they needed. What did he care what happened to his sperm? It wasn't as if he was going to ever get to fuck anyone. Why did they have to fight when they had to know that they would never win?

Tim had said that this was probably the last time they would try and get a viable donation from Eight. He'd said donation as if it had a choice in the matter of whether or not they took it. Simon felt the grin that always came to his face when he thought of Tim. He was a force to be reckoned with. Of course he was a Grade-A Prick, but he was a forceful prick.

The second they got off the elevator they could feel the animals down there. Especially Seven and Nine. They looked human, but they were all nothing but animals to him and the other men who worked there. When they stood in front of Eight's cage a kind of energy poured from the cell next door and Simon, called Phillip back then, knew that Nine was up to its tricks again. Scott went to the door and pounded on it with a club

"Zulu Alpha Nine, you come out where I can see you now. Don't make me have to come in there and get you again. I won't be as easy this time."

Scott turned to him and grinned. Scott was a sadistic bastard and he loved to cause pain to the donors. Actually, he liked to cause pain to everything, including his family. When Nine answered Simon felt a kind of fear run up his spine.

"Come in and try. I'm not bleeding this time and I'll feed on your hot blood. I could always use a nice snack before I kill you."

Simon believed it too. He nearly told Scott not to go in, but he was armed with a Taser and a gun. Simon gave him the thumbs up and watched as he entered the cage. When he heard Scott scream then it abruptly cut off Simon knew a kind of fear that he'd never felt before. Suddenly, out of the cage came a huge panther, its coat a silky black and teeth that looked razor sharp.

As the cat leapt at John he pulled Eight in front of him. As soon as both men were down the cat seemed to push Eight away from her so that she could reach the neck of John. She bit down hard on his throat and tore it away.

With blood still dripping from her muzzle she started to track them, herding them, Simon realized, until they were standing close together. He could smell that one of them had pissed himself. Simon couldn't blame him; he was nearly to that point himself. Circling around to the right, the cat growled low and deep in its throat.

"You'll back off, Nine; I'll kill you if you don't. I thought we were getting along so well for the past two weeks." Simon tried to reason with her. He so didn't want to die. "Now, be a good girl and go into your cell and we'll forget this ever happened."

"Just fucking kill her," Tim screamed at him. That's when Simon remembered he had a gun in his hand too. "That's what you're supposed to do when they go bad. Kill her and get this over with."

When Simon drew his gun to fire the big cat leapt through the air at him. Its jaws clamped around his hand and, with a hard bite, his hand came off with the gun still in his fingers. Blood spurted everywhere as it spit the appendage and gun out of its mouth. Simon didn't remember anything much after that. He tried to crawl away, but he knew that he had to stop the bleeding or he would die down there. And that cat would more than likely eat him. Wrapping his tie around his forearm Simon prayed that someone would find him before it was too late.

He was in a lab again when he woke, though not like the one he'd been in before. There was an IV in his arm and his other, the one the cat had bitten, was wrapped in white gauze, blood spattered along it. He started to move and his body hurt.

"You're going to feel odd for a few days. It's the fae blood I had them give you. It's made you an immortal. Not a true immortal like me, but one nonetheless. You're very welcome."

Simon looked over at the man in the large chair by the window. Sherman. Sherman had saved him. Then he realized what he'd said. "Fae? I'm an immortal? I don't think...I don't understand."

"You were too near death for me to just let you lay there and try to make it to the hospital. And my mate was coming down the elevator. I had to get you out of there before she was able to make you whole and read your mind. If that would have happened then she would have known everything I have planned, and I can't have that happen. No, this was better. You'll be able to live a very long time provided that you don't piss me off too much and we can work on the combination of DNA together."

Simon looked at Sherman. Partners? He wanted them to work together as partners. Simon lay back on the bed and looked at the man. Simon knew that he knew about as much about DNA research as any high school student. He'd only been pretending that he was helping when all he'd been doing was mimicking what the others had said when he was asked. But he knew that if he told Sherman this then his immortality and his partnership would be gone. Besides, he was making great money at fifty-two dollars a week, and maybe he could ask for a raise. A man making that kind of money in the thirties was either a bootlegger or a thief.

Simon nodded that he would help the other men as before. It wasn't until days later that he found out that he was the sole survivor and that he would be the one running the lab. He'd been able to fake things along and even had Sherman bring in more lab guys. That was fine with Simon. And the fancy new equipment was fun too.

~~~

Zane was moving the heavy engine to the belly of the SUV when Danny came into the bay area. He looked so relieved to be back to work that she smiled at him. The package that had been left at the garage had turned out to be nothing more than a sample someone had sent to her to try and get her to order their products. The *mechanic* had been just that, the mechanic that had worked on his car.

"The guy that owns this car called again. He is a real pain in my hind end. He's claiming that you did something to his vehicle and that's why the engine seized up. I told him if he had legitimate proof of the oil changes that he'd made then I would take full responsibility for the engine. Said he'd get back with me. What a wiener head."

Zane burst out laughing. Danny never cursed. Not in all the time she'd known him had he ever said anything but "mother pots," or some other version of that. To hear him say hind end and wiener head all in the same day was a rarity that she was going to savor. The guy must have really pissed him off.

"I can have this finished by tomorrow afternoon, but if he is bitching about it that much, do you want me to stop?"

In a way she really wanted him to say stop, but it would drive both of them nuts to leave a job half finished. She knew that as well as he did. But he looked very tempted. Finally he just shook his head and told her no. "If it ain't ready when we said it would be then he may not pay anyway. If I have to sell it to recoup my money, that wouldn't be ideal, but I could do it. Put'er in, Zane, and we'll sort it out when he calls back."

She agreed. People like the owner were always trying to take advantage of someone else and she didn't want Danny to have to eat the cost of the engine. But he was right; a nice ride like this one, he'd have no problems selling for more than he had in it.

Zane was just finishing up for the afternoon when the phone rang in the office. She had never answered it before and didn't even pause in her work when she heard it. Danny was still on it when her pager went off. Without glancing at the number, she went to the pay phone. Danny was walking toward her with a piece of paper in his hand when the man at the other end answered.

"I have a sanctioned job for you. The queen would like to know if you can meet with her before you leave to fulfill it? She said that it is very important."

Zane took the sheet of paper from Danny and with a quick read, leaned back against the wall. Aaron MacManus needed to meet with her too. Would this life ever...well, it couldn't now unless she could get the queen to—

"Do you think she could meet me at the MacManus'? I have to talk to someone there as well. And tell her that I have something I need from her, a...a favor."

"Yes, miss, I can tell her that. She will not be overjoyed by it, but I will ask her. Also, the package, would you like for me to send it to the master's home? I can send it to either place."

Zane was startled by the request. As far as she knew this man worked for the queen and was in that realm. That he knew the master was a little scary. But she didn't have time to speculate about it now. She told him that would be fine and hung up. Calling the MacManus home proved to be a little more difficult.

"This is the MacManus residence, Mac MacManus speaking. How may I direct your call?"

The kid couldn't have been much more than pre-teen. His mouthful of a greeting had startled Zane, so much so that she didn't respond for several seconds and had the kid repeating his speech.

"I need to speak to…did your parents actually call you Mac as in Mac MacManus?" She hadn't meant to ask, but it was just too strange not to. He laughed at her question and told her that his real name was different, but they called him that for other reasons. She had to give the master points, he was being careful about using his and his family's name.

"Good job, kid. Is your dad around? I need to speak to him. Tell him that he called and left a message to talk to me."

"Sure. But he's with my mom. They are having a…we're not allow to tell people they are fighting again, but they are having a really loud discussion about my sister Li…my sister."

The famous Lizzy, Zane was sure. She wondered if she really did make a noise like a car out of alignment when she didn't get her way. Having met her mother Zane was sure she was fairly close. Zane waited until the master came to the phone. His voice sounded like he was still a little pissed.

"Miss Zander. I was wondering if you could please come by and talk with me for a few minutes after you finish work? I have a couple of things I'd like to discuss with you and a few more that I need to clarify. It shouldn't take all that long."

"Sure, and it's Zane. I have to meet with the queen too so I hope you don't mind that I'm meeting her there too. I need to…I have something I have to do later and it would speed things up if I didn't have to go to Molavonta too." She knew she should have asked first, but it had been a really strange call and then his note.

"Of course. I would imagine that you and Aiden have plans for this evening as well. I remember when…hell, Sara and I still go at it like sex-starved maniacs. What time should I tell him you'll be here?"

Zane didn't even think about Aiden. It wasn't like he hadn't been on her mind all day, but she didn't think about making arrangements with him or even telling him what she had to do tonight. She was still thinking about it when Aaron spoke again.

"You didn't tell him. Zane, you are an important part of his life. You and he will need to—"

"Look, MacManus, when I want you to meddle in my life I'll let you have at it after your queen. Right now I'm making arrangements to meet with you because you requested it. That in no way, shape, or form gives you any rights to my personal life. You know, you people really need to get a life if all you have to do is screw around in others'. I'll be at your house in an hour."

She hung up. It was bad enough that she felt guilty that she hadn't thought of telling Aiden, but these people didn't have to rub it into her face too. She was nearly out the door when she had to return and clean up her tools. Damned man nearly made her forget the most fun she had all day, cleaning up and organizing her tools. Shifting to her panther just on the outskirts of town Zane moved along the perimeter of the city limits until she was about a mile from their home.

The first dart hit her in the shoulder and made her stagger. The second hit her in the hip and she could feel the effects racing though her body in seconds. By the time the third hit her in the hip again, she was going down. She reached out as quickly as she could and found Aiden.

"Drugged. Can't talk. Listen. One mile northwest of the driveway. Don't follow. Dangerous." Then everything went black.

CHAPTER 21

Aiden paced. He didn't know what else to do but to pace. It had been two hours and he felt as if the entire world had slowed just to annoy him. He wanted to go after her, go out to where she said she was and find her, beat her ass, then make love to her all night. He glared at the queen once again.

"Listen here, young man. If I wanted a man to look at me all pissed off the way you are right now I could have stayed home. As it is I've got Shamus driving me insane because he is under the misguided impression that I need him to hound my every waking hour. Sit down."

There was just enough compulsion in her voice to make him sit. He wasn't any happier with sitting across from her than he'd been pacing the room and he wanted to make sure she knew it. "She said that she'd been drugged. I could go and see if I can find her based on the location she gave me. I want you to take these fucking..." Aiden took a deep breath. "Please take the hold off the doors so that I may leave. Please."

"Better. Much better. At least you left the threats out this time, but still no dice. You stay here until I know what is going on. I can't let you run...Duncan, how does the saying go? I can't let you run how?"

Aiden was going to scream. Who cared about a stupid saying? He was about to stand again when she simply looked at him with a raised brow.

"I believe it is 'run about willing kneeling,' mistress. Master Aiden, would you care for some refreshments? Miss Penny has made a delightful can of pie with a heavy cream. Though I have not figured out how this particular cream has any more weight to it than the milk I purchase for the children. I can bring you some if you like."

Aiden stared at Duncan. He rested his head on his fist and simply stared at him. There was no hope for it, Aiden was locked in an asylum and they'd thrown away the key.

"It's run about willy nilly. And canapé, not can of pie. Cream is heavier because...you know, I don't care. Please let me go and find—"

The door from outside opened in the spacious kitchen and in walked Bradley and his mate Airic. Aiden groaned. More people, and why the fuck could they come in and he couldn't go out? He stood up to go while the door was still open. He was nearly there when Aaron spoke up behind him.

"If you go out that door I will drain you. She said to wait. And you will wait. And will you stop that infernal pacing? Christ, you people walk all the time. When was the last time any of you just sat down and worked a problem out by thinking? All this back and forth makes me dizzy."

Aiden looked at Aaron. Aiden decided that he had to die first, right after the queen. He was going to make them suffer too. He started going over a list of things he was going to do to them both when he felt the first small touch of Zane. He had to sit down quickly. Everyone in the room, including the children, stopped and started at him.

"Aiden, I'm at my lair. Can you...do you remember how to get here? I'm still a little fuzzy, but I'm getting much better. I have some information for everyone, but I need you to come here first. I need t...I need to feed from you. Can I do that?"

"Of course, love. I'll be right...you will need to tell the queen. She is holding me prisoner here until I hear from you and I'm not sure she will take my word that you have contacted me."

Aiden knew the exact moment that she had contacted the queen. Mel looked relieved and a little pissed. Aiden wondered what Zane had said to her. It would have been great to have been a part of that conversation.

"She is at her lair and is waiting on you. Though I'm half tempted to keep you here out of spite. That woman can try my patience more than any one person I know. Go. And I expect you both back here in an hour. No screwing around and I mean it."

Aiden left the kitchen and was standing next to Zane's bed in a moment. He had the ability to materialize wherever he was needed for very long distances, as all of his family did. But only so long as he'd been given permission to enter a home could he go there. He looked down at her.

There were small injuries to her shoulder he could see from what appeared to be small puncture marks. He wanted to look over her entire body, but for now he was just happy to see her. He lay down next to her on the big bed and pulled her into his arms.

"You really all right? I was so worried about you that I wasn't sure what to think. Do you know who did this?"

"No. Please, I need you so badly. You can make the poison run out of my system faster by letting me feed."

Aiden turned toward her and pulled her close. Her body felt cooled, almost cold to him. When he felt her tongue run across his vein he groaned and his cock hardened. As soon as her fangs sank into his flesh he rolled her over to her back and covered her with his body, warming her as best he could. Her answering moan made him glad they were lying down. He was sure he'd not have stood long with her doing the things she was doing to him and feeding.

When she pulled back after licking the tiny wounds closed. Aiden looked down at her. She already looked better. Her cheeks where rosy and her lips, pale before, were a deep pink. Aiden couldn't help himself; he leaned down and captured her lower lip with his teeth.

"The queen said we only have an hour to get back to her and the others. I'm not sure what she would do to us if we were late, but I'd certainly like to find out if you're up to it." He rocked into her soft folds.

"Hummm, I'm not sure she can…oh yes, again."

He moved again, this time with more pressure to her pussy. His cock ached to be released. Released from his tightening pants, then pounding deep into her. Zane wrapped her arms around his neck and pulled him closer as she ran her feet down his naked calves. She had removed their clothes again.

"I love that trick. I think that is by and far the most useful thing you can do." He moved until his cock was just at her entrance. "I'm not going to take my time with this, love. I need to fuck you hard and fast. I need to spill my seed deep into your pussy."

For an answer Zane moved up as he entered her. Her heat wrapped around him tightly and he felt the ripple of her body adjusting to his. It made him shudder with profound need. But he wanted more this time. He wanted to take her deeper. Pulling out, she whimpered and wrapped her legs tight around his hips.

"I want you from behind. Sit up and roll over. I want your sweet ass up here where I can fuck that tight hole with my finger while I fuck this pussy of yours hard."

Zane rolled over quickly and before she could move to her knees, he wrapped his arm around her waist and pulled her back and up with his right arm. He had his cock ready to take her the moment she was where he wanted her to be. With one driving push, he was seated deep inside of her.

"Christ, you're hot. Put your head down, baby, and hang on. I can't wait any longer."

Gripping her hips and pulling her back to him, Aiden held her still as he pulled out to the tip of his engorged cock then slammed into her. Over and over he did this until sweat poured down his back and over his eyes. Leaning over, he ran his fingers over her hard clit, gathered her cream, and brought his hand to her ass. Holding her ass cheeks open, he massaged her cream all over her tight pucker until he was sure she was wet enough. This time, instead of working her up by stretching her, he plunged his finger deep. He stopped when her cry echoed around the room.

"Please, Aiden, don't stop. I beg you. More, I need more." He couldn't stop now, not when she needed him.

Moving deep into both her pussy and ass Aiden started a rhythm of in one place and out the other, keeping her filled with him over and over. When he moved a second finger into her she didn't even slow her backward push, but pressed herself harder against him with each movement. Aiden wanted her to come, needed her to come with all he was.

Pulling out of her ass he leaned over her inert body and rested his hands on either side of her shoulders. He had the leverage he needed to take her even faster. When she bared her neck for him, Aiden nuzzled deep and, with a quick swipe of his tongue, bit. Her climax rippled along her body inside and out. His cock felt strangled for a moment then she started to pull him deeper. His own climax roared though him so quickly that he was breathless with it. Sealing the prick marks Aiden collapsed on top of her and decided if he were to die right now, he'd die a very happy vampire. Rolling over, he pulled her with him.

"Mel is pissed. She said that she hoped we enjoyed ourselves while everyone was waiting on us."

Aiden chuckled. "And what did you tell her? It was no doubt very sorrowful and full of remorse."

Zane snorted. "I told her that if she got fucked more often she'd be in a much better mood and to leave us alone. She said she was going to make you a eunuch if you didn't obey her."

Aiden felt his cock twitch at that thought. Before he could comment on that and have them hurrying to the mansion, Zane spoke again.

"I told her she could try, but Shamus would be suffering right along with you. She said she would leave all your manly parts alone."

~~~

Simon moved along the room again. He was livid and he wanted to make sure that the idiots with him were very aware of it.

He tossed another dagger at the wolf currently tied up on the wall. The blades weren't silver so the fool would live through it...so long as Simon didn't hit his heart, but he was going to make sure the next time he sent them on a mission they fucking did what he wanted.

"You claim you hit her, yet still there is no body to bring back to me. What the hell am I supposed to believe, that she disappeared? That some...I don't know, creature from the black lagoon took her into his hidey hole and hid her from you? A body just doesn't disappear no matter what you think. If you had hit her as many times as you said, then her body would fucking"—he threw another knife—"be"—then another—"there." This one came very close to his beating heart.

Simon turned and leaned on the desk. He was furious and he was nearly at the breaking point of killing everything in the lab and anywhere else he could find someone to kill. Taking several deep breaths, he stayed there until he thought he was back under enough control so as not to take anymore lives today.

"Get that piece of shit out of my sight." The second wolf jumped to do what Simon wanted. "I want patrols up and down that street twenty-four-seven until you either find a body or you find her. I want her found and I don't give a shit how you do it."

The wolf turned and looked at Simon. He didn't know why, but he just knew whatever was going to spew from his mouth was going to piss Simon off again and he wasn't sure he would be able to keep himself from murdering him. Taking a deep breath again Simon raised his hand to stop the wolf.

"If you value your miserable life, you will not say or ask whatever it is you're thinking. I will kill you and him if you do."

The wolf seemed to contemplate it, but in the end left the room. He was carrying his friend over his shoulder as he walked out the door. Simon watched them, waiting, or maybe even hoping, that he would decide to ask whatever it was anyway so that he could kill them both. When the door shut, Simon sat down and pulled the folder to him.

Two days ago he'd gotten a call from someone that Sherman had trusted telling Simon that Zulu Alpha Nine was alive. He didn't believe him and told the man that he needed more proof than his word. Today a thick file showed up at his home. Inside it was not only what *it* had been doing since the lab incident, but also pictures. And not all of them of Zulu Alpha Nine, but also of *its* "work" that *it* had been doing.

It was an assassin. And by the pictures *it* was a damned brutal one too. The file didn't say who *it* worked for, nor did it say how this person had gotten the information but it was *it* all right.

There was also information saying that it was working for or associated with the MacManuses. He wanted to hit something again at that. He'd been trying to get that Sara person for several weeks now and killing her husband was proving to be just as hard as finding *it*. He wondered briefly if *it* had anything to do with that and dismissed that quickly. *It* had never been that smart in the first place. A lucky chance that *it* had gotten him at all as far as he was concerned.

Moving along to the business side of his desk Simon pulled out the photo of it. Beautiful. That was all he could think to call it. Tossing it back to the open file he watched as the cleaning crew came in and cleaned up the mess that the wolf had made on the floor.

Things were not going well. Not well at all, as a matter of fact. There was no money left, at least none that he was willing to let go of. There was very little left in the way of jewels too. Sherman had told him that they were from the throne chair that he'd resided in when he had been in the castle. Simon had never believed there was a queen, much less a castle, but had prudently kept his mouth shut about that. Sherman had a mean temper and Simon never wanted to be on the receiving end of that again.

Pulling out the bottom drawer to the desk, he looked at the ten rubies and the six emeralds that were left. Not a lot. He had to find a way to make more money or he would have to give up his house and car very soon. No matter how much he'd tried to persuade the idiot landlord, there just wasn't any way to convince him that the money would soon be pouring in. Of course Simon had been saying that for the past five years so maybe he should come up with another line or just move. But moving required cash, which was where the issue was to begin with.

That's why he needed to get that Sara person. He really wanted to get his hands on Mel the bitch—Simon had never thought of her as anything but the name Sherman had given her so it had stuck. Selling Mel would be the most profitable, but she was powerful and if Simon was honest with himself, she was a tad scary. No, he needed to find a way to get Sara, or at the very least Zulu Alpha Nine. No hope for it, he thought, he was going to have to do it himself. Picking up the phone he dialed the phone number just in front of him.

"Hello, my name is P. Simon Sinclair. You need to put that MacManus person on the phone now. I have something I would like to propose to him."

Yes, Simon thought, *a very nice proposal. Give me your wife or I kill you.* When the man who answered the phone asked him to please wait, Simon figured the Sara person would be in his hands by nightfall.

CHAPTER 22

Aaron and Aiden were just about to go into the living room when Duncan came out of the kitchen. He had a very odd look on his face and nearly walked past them. Aaron knew that something had upset the man and waited for him to gather his thoughts.

"A very rude man is requesting...no, sire, he is demanding that you come to the phone. He believes that he has a proposal for you to discuss. I do not believe that he is human. There is evil...or something that I can feel though the phone lines. I do not like this one bit."

Several years ago, Mel had given Duncan a boost to his telepathic powers. The man had a very good sixth sense about people when he met them, but never any more than a person to person ability. Then one afternoon someone had called and Duncan had been hurt when he'd met the man for an issue that the stranger said Aaron had set up. Now Duncan knew when someone was lying and also when they were not quite human, even when on the phone. Everyone loved Duncan, and with good reason; the man didn't have a mean bone in his body.

"Is he still on the phone? And what is it he said he wanted?" Aaron started toward the kitchen to answer the phone, when suddenly Aiden stopped him. His eyes had turned and Aaron could see his fangs had dropped. Aaron stilled.

"Don't. Zane is coming now. She said to wait for her. Something is off and she said that you must wait."

Aaron hadn't lived this long to ignore things he didn't understand. So he waited. Looking over at Duncan, Aaron saw that he looked relieved. Almost as if he knew that whatever was going on was now going to be resolved.

Zane came into the kitchen as a spectrum. It was quite a sight and one that Aaron was glad he'd witnessed. She just faded into the room, but not completely in a solid form. She was on an assignment, she said.

"The man on the phone, who is it? Do you know his name, Mr. Duncan?"

"Oh, yes, miss. He said that he was P. Simon Sinclair. I hope you do not mind that I had the queen contact you. I had a feeling he was connected to you in some way."

"Sinclair is the person from the other day, Master MacManus. He is the person who shot up your home and tried to harm you. I don't know how he got your name, but it is imperative that you do not give him anything more. I can't be there for another few hours yet."

Aaron burned with anger. This was the person who, without Zane's help, would have shot Sara and had kidnapped little Emma. He felt his mate coming toward him and wondered if she was safe even now.

"Tell me what I can do to end this. This man, this person, is going to die and I for one would like it to be sooner rather than later."

Zane grinned. Then she looked away from them. He could tell that this was draining on her, being here in the semi-flesh, and wanted to tell her to come back now. But he could see that she was a determined woman and would not intercede. As of yet anyway.

"Talk to him, but tell him nothing. I need to know what he says and what sort of information he has now. I have to...my target is on the move and I have to finish this. If you would allow Aiden to listen in I will be able to get the information from him."

Aiden didn't look any happier about Zane not being here than Aaron did and wondered if he had any knowledge that she had left him. Thinking that these two would have a very hard time of it if they didn't give a little, Aaron reached out and put his hand on Aiden's forearm when he felt the anger boil from him.

"I would speak to you, Zane St. James," Aiden practically growled at her. "There is a matter of you leaving here without permission. I thought we had agreed that if you went on an assignment, I would accompany you."

"No. You said you were going and I said that you weren't. There was no agreement between us, you stubborn jackass. And when or even if I need your permission to do anything will be a cold day in hell. I'll be back in a few hours provided you don't manage to piss me off anymore than you have already." Then she was gone.

Aaron tried not to laugh. He really did, but it was just too funny to watch the big vamp standing next to him try to regain control of his temper. Aaron thought that Aiden would need to curb his tongue if he ever thought to have a mate he could live with.

"Like you do yours, Aaron, my love? How long do you suppose it was before you finally figured out that demands and threats don't work with the women of this Kiss?" Sara whispered though his mind.

"Too long, I'm afraid. But this girl, this woman, she is stronger than Aiden, I believe. He will be fighting with her for a great many years if he doesn't learn it soon."

"Hummm, I'm not worried. They will come to a happy medium soon. He loves her." Aaron felt her love warm his body as he moved to the phone. *"I wonder if he's told her yet."*

Aaron had wondered the same thing as he pushed the mute button on the phone. *"I doubt it. Zane doesn't strike me as a romantic type."*

"This is MacManus. How may I help you?" Duncan had said the man had asked for MacManus, not Master or Aaron. And Aaron wasn't going to give him any more information than necessary.

"This is P. Simon Sinclair. I would like to know if you are aware that your wife and I have been having an affair for years? I want her for myself and am willing to take her off your hands. Now. Today, if possible."

Aaron pulled the phone from his ear and looked at it. He was wondering if the man was serious or simply that stupid. Aaron decided that he was both. "No, I wasn't aware of that. How long has this been going on, did you say? I don't believe that I've ever heard her say your name before, not even in the throes of passion. And she can be very vocal when she hits her peak. Are you sure it's my wife?"

Aiden chuckled and Aaron nearly joined him. This man was arrogant, he'd give him that. His shuddered reply nearly had Aaron laugh out loud.

"Pass...I don't think...I would hope that she...Christ. I need a moment." Aaron could hear the paper shuffle close to the phone before P. Simon came back. "Yes. Throes of passion notwithstanding, we are having an affair. I've asked her several times to leave you, but she seems to think you won't give her up. Man to man, I would ask that of you now."

"Ask him to meet you, sire. Tell him that your wife is out of town and you would like for him to meet you somewhere. Not at the house," Zane whispered though his mind.

"Why don't I meet you somewhere? I'm assuming that she isn't with you right now and really out of town visiting her cousin. We can discuss your plans for providing for her. My wife, she has expensive tastes as I'm sure you have found out."

"That would be fine. Out of town, you say? Do you know when she'll be returning and how? I would like to talk to her before we have our little talk. I'm sure you understand."

"Of course. She is supposed to return tomorrow night. I pick her up at the bus station downtown. Insisted on riding a bus, of all things. How about you and I meet on Tuesday morning, the day after she comes home?"

"Yes, yes. That would be fine. I'll see you then. Thanks, MacManus. You won't regret this. Not at all."

Aaron hung up a minute later and looked over at his mate. She looked so beautiful and if she thought for one second that she was going to be anywhere near that bus station tomorrow night he was going to beat her pretty little ass but hard. Thinking of her pretty ass made his cock jerk to attention. When she smiled at him he couldn't tell if she knew his thoughts or that he wanted her again. Either way, he was sure that pain was going to be involved.

"You can bet your sweet ass there will be." Her smile made his cock settle down. She could be very scary when she wanted to be.

~~~

Zane moved along the wall of the house. The target, a vampire of great age, was somewhere ahead of her and she had lost just enough concentration a few minutes ago that he'd been able to hurt her. Holding her hand over the bleeding wound at her side she poured magic into it to stop the bleeding.

Damn it, this was Simon's fault. Well, not all of it. Some of it was Aiden's too. The nerve of the man thinking she would just roll over and play the simpering mate because he had said so. What did he think she'd been doing all these years before he came along? Sitting in a padded room waiting to be taken care of? Stupid, arrogant asswipe. When she got back to him she was going to show him the meaning of obey and permission.

The vampire moved to the opposite wall. She couldn't see him, but she knew precisely where he was. A part of her magic made her able to see beyond the shadows he pulled about him.

"Dillon Nickolas Anderson, by order of the Vampire Council I am hereby ordered to terminate your life. It has been deemed that you have become a rogue and that your crimes against humanity make this warrant of death executable."

"Join me." His voice, rough with his beast, echoed across the barren room.

"As good as that sounds I think I'll have to refuse. I have something to do later and it requires me to be living. Sorry. Do you have anything to say on your own behalf?"

"Join me or die."

The blast of heat barely missed her. Had she not leaned to her right, it would have hit her full in the chest. As it was, she had a nice scorch mark on her arm. They had told her he was old and that his powers were only transportation and a little ability to move across space quickly. This heat of fire was something she'd never encountered before in a vampire.

The first blade she had pulled hit him in the arm and pinned him to the wall. She could smell the acidity of his blackened blood immediately. The second blade hit him in the chest, just shy of his heart. Pulling a stack of stars from her neckline, she tossed several of them at him and hit his hands, left thigh, and his ear. They were deep enough that she knew he was stuck where he was. She pulled her blade from her back and walked toward him as she finished her order.

"I have been foreordained to remove your head and then to annihilate your body until you no longer exist. This is by order of the Vampire Council of the Ninth District of the Realm of Chicago."

Her blade whispered through the air and through his body at the neck. His head, handsome even in his beastly state, hung onto his shoulders for several seconds before it tilted forward and then landed on the floor between her feet. Zane didn't look down at it. She didn't want to see it die or the accusations it would toss at her long before it closed its eyes.

Dillon's body began to burn first. Smoke began to steam from his body then more as the seconds ticked by. Because he was so old it would take longer to turn to ash than a younger vampire. When he was nearly too hot for her to watch his body simply *poofed*, leaving a pile of ash and clothes where a man had once been. His head, mostly bone, followed the same pattern only seconds later.

Zane walked to the windows in the front of the house and lifted a window. As soon as a nice breeze circulated through the house it began to pick up the remains and take them out with it on the breeze. Leaving through the same window Zane shifted to a hawk and made her way to the moonlit night sky.

Her body felt heavy, almost too heavy for flight. And tired. Zane was tired of what she was and what she did. There were more deaths on her head than most full scale armies could account for in a single battle. She wanted it finished and as soon as she thought of that, she thought of the MacManus home and Simon contacting them. Then it wasn't long before her thoughts turned to Aiden.

She wasn't angry with him anymore. Well, at least not *as* angry with him. She didn't want him to order her around, but she could see why he thought he might need to. She was reckless and her job, this one anyway, was dangerous. If she were to get too hurt he'd not be able to feed, and as much as Zane wanted to think otherwise, she knew that that, above all else, was why he needed her. She wasn't stupid enough to believe that he would want her for anything else. Unless it was the sex, which was extremely enjoyable.

Zane wasn't sure what she thought of him. He was nice enough, she supposed. Actually, other than the stubborn arrogant way he acted all the time he was really nice. She had to smile at that because she knew he probably thought the same things about her.

Moving along the sky toward her lair Zane saw the world below her in a different view than she had before. While the colors were not as bright as they were when she was human, they still looked more...well, more, she supposed. There were wolves playing below her and their scent called to her. She saw the plants differently too. For as much as she wanted to believe it was the moonlight she knew it was Aiden and his mating with her. And just like that he was moving through her mind.

"I'm sorry I pissed you off earlier. I didn't...that's not true. I did mean what I said. But I worry about you. I know in my head that you can take care of yourself, hell, take care of all of us, but I need to protect you."

"I'm not used to answering to anyone but the queen. She and I...well, we don't always get along. I guess I could be more—I'm not stupid, you know. I know enough to come in out of the rain and not to take on more than I can handle." Which was almost true, but she did try. She could feel his laughter at that and wanted to

yell again. Instead, she took a deep breath and spoke again. *"Are you always going to be this irritating?"*

"Probably. But you must admit I'm not boring." She laughed at him. *"Where are you, love? Are you close to the mansion?"*

"Still in Chicago. I should be home in another few hours. I was just enjoying the night and flying high in the sky. Why? Is there something wrong?"

"No. Nothing wrong. Let me come to you. I can be there in a few seconds. I'd very much like to spend some time with you."

Did she want that too? To spend some time with him outside of his lair? She wasn't sure, but told him to come to her anyway. When he appeared below her seconds later she dropped to the ground and shifted to herself. He smiled at her and her heart flipped.

"You make that seem so easy, so fluid. And I can't hold my animal for long, maybe a couple of hours. How will I learn to shift like you do and not feel like my bones are breaking?"

She simply stared at him. He could do what she did. Shift, talk to the earth, and—

"How do you know that you can't shift like me? I mean, you have my weapons and you've used some of the things I've transferred to you. Have you tried to shift and hold it?"

She could tell by the look on his face that he had not. She walked around him and tried to see him as anything more than the panther he'd been before. She knew that he could be a hawk; he had those memories in his mind.

"I guess I haven't. Even when we're together, you sort of overwhelm me with your ability. I guess I've never given it much thought as to what I can do with what you've given me." He put his hands on her shoulders and held her away from him. "I have to concentrate on my animal like—"

He was suddenly a large black cat. Zane couldn't help but laugh at the shocked expression on the panther's face. "I think you have that down."

"It was as fluid as you. I mean, Christ, there wasn't even the slightest bit of pain. Usually when I shift to something I've never

178

been before, it's painful even for me." He rubbed his large head against her leg as he continued. *"I'd very much like for you to shift into your cat and let me have my wicked way with you."*

She was tempted, but in the end told him no. "We have things to do with your master and playing in this field will not only get us into trouble, but could likely have us darted as escaped animals from the zoo." She rubbed his fur. "Now shift to something small. A house mouse."

"Will I have to be human first?" She felt the energy as he asked. *"Can I go from this to whatever I want in the same way?"*

"Yes. You might find it necessary to shrink to something smaller quickly. I've used it to go through cracks in walls and then become something larger if need be." She watched the fur along his arms shift to a lighter color and then he was a tiny mouse.

He shifted into several animals in a very short time. She could feel his hunger but without her being up to par, which she nearly was, she couldn't feed him. When they took to the sky she knew that her life was forever changed.

CHAPTER 23

Aiden didn't want to do anything but take Zane against the nearest hard surface and pound his cock deep inside of her. But they had to get ready for tonight. He was sure if he didn't at least show her he could be helpful she would leave him at home and go off on her own.

He knew that the other weapons were on his hips and the ones along his body. She'd told him that he would be able to be dressed and pull them. He'd wondered about that and was glad to know he didn't have to remove his pants to use them. But being able to shift and to hold it, he knew that this was probably the greatest thing he'd gotten from her. Besides her as his mate.

When she'd reached up and pulled her own blade from her back he watched her as she moved. She was fluid in this as well, moving gracefully though the grass as though it was second nature for her to swing a heavy blade. This, too, was something he needed to learn. The way that she moved, the way that she made everything she did seem a part of her rather than simply a weapon she used. He came up behind her and wrapped his body to hers.

"Show me, Allison. Show me how to dance with my sword so that I can help you when you need me."

When she stretched out her arms with her blade in her right hand he moved along them with his arms against her. His blade now in his left, he touched her but didn't crowd her as she moved.

"The blade, like all the others, will be an extension of your arm. Just as you use your ability to shift, you'll need to be proficient in this as well. You will need only to think about it, where you want it to go, what you need it to extinguish. Your thought is its command."

Aiden felt it then, the connection. It was a part of him, like the opening and closing of his hand. The sword moved in precise movements that looked like he knew what he was doing. He grinned. Good thing one of them did.

"Don't think about it as a sword but as your hand. See what it does? I can toss my blade in the air." Suddenly, hers was flying across the forest and embedded deep into the ground. "Then I need only to ask for its return and I have it." The blade came at them in a spinning motion, pommel over blade until it landed in her hand again pommel first.

"Christ." He hadn't moved away from her when it came at them and was glad that he hadn't. He would never have felt the power of its return to her body otherwise.

Aiden took a deep breath and asked his blade to land where hers had. There was a small tingle in his arm then the blade was in the ground.

Zane had turned and looked up at him a smile so radiant that his breath caught. Aiden suddenly realized he was in love. In love with his mate. Cupping the back of her head, he brought her mouth to his for a kiss.

As far as kisses went it was quick, but it was powerful. Her answering moan rumbled through his body and it was everything he could do not to turn her into the shelter of his arms and take them to the ground. He pulled away and leaned his forehead onto hers.

"You are by and far a major distraction to me, but one that I'm looking forward to spending the rest of my life with. I love you, Allison. I know that my timing could be better, but I really love you."

The look in her eyes made him pause. She looked terrified for several seconds then she looked away. He started to ask her what was wrong when she spoke.

"I don't know what I feel about you. I've never...you know what I am, what I'm capable of, yet you still say that. I'm...no one has ever loved me before, or I them. I'm not saying I won't love you. I just...I don't know how."

Aiden decided he could live with that, for now. She hadn't said she hated him and to him that was better than he expected a few days ago. He had willed his sword back to him and it was safely in his hand before he thought about what he'd done. But apparently Zane didn't. She laughed outright and turned to give him a hug—the first one she had ever given him, or anyone that he knew of, since she'd met him.

When they landed at the master's home he felt better. Hungry, but better. When they entered the household Duncan was there was a packet of blood for them both as well as a steak, nearly raw for Zane.

"The young miss was injured sire. I felt as if she would benefit more from this than you would." Duncan was a treasure, Aiden thought, and shook the man's hand.

~~~

Simon set up men at each door at the bus terminal at two in the afternoon. He didn't want to take the chance of missing that Sara person by her coming home early and him not getting her. He couldn't believe how incredibly stupid her husband was to give out the information on when she was going to arrive and that she was driving home. The meeting with Aaron would be the topping on the cake and his idea to kill the vampire was all planned out.

"If you miss her then not only will I cut you to pieces, but your entire family will become donors for my next projects. I won't tolerate failure again, do you understand me?"

The wolf standing before him was new. He'd come to him late last night looking for a place to sleep and had killed three of Simon's best men before settling down on a pallet near the fire. Simon asked him to come to him first thing this morning and he'd made him in charge of the mission.

"I will serve you as you deserve. The men are at each gate waiting. I've given them the picture of the target and they also know that failure will not be an option. That if they miss her I will kill them, but not before they watch me kill their young."

Simon knew he'd made the best choice. This man was a brutal killer and he was huge too. Simon thought maybe he might have to get some of his sperm and see if he could breed more just like him. Dismissing him Simon settled down at the table and looked over the new plans for the lab.

Sara was going to be the golden goose. Not only was she going to carry the seeds of his future child—he'd only just decided that—but she was also going to be the mother of all the army he was putting together. He mentally rubbed his hands together in anticipation. Yes, he was close, closer than he'd been all those decades ago when Tim was in charge.

It was four o'clock when he started for the mall. He didn't want to miss the look on MacManus' face when he realized that his wife wasn't coming home to him and that he was going to die as well. Simon had three men already set up at the mall to subdue the vampire and was confident that things were going as planned. When he got to the restaurant at a little before five he sat in the corner near the entrance to watch for the vamp. Simon wasn't really sure what he looked like, but knew without a doubt that he'd be able to pick the stupid man out without any problems. It was nearly an hour later when he realized that the vamp didn't know what he looked like either and could very well be sitting at one of the tables right now waiting for him. Simon pulled out his cell phone just as it rang.

"I'm running a bit behind. I just realized that I haven't a clue that I'm looking for and was wondering if you could please give me a description of maybe what you have on to help me out once I get there?"

Simon grinned. Okay, give the man points for thinking like he did. "Of course. I should have thought of that first. I have on a navy blue polo and gray dress slacks. I have dark hair and I'm sitting near the place that sells those delicious pretzels."

Simon looked down at the napkins in front of him. He'd had six of them since he'd sat down and wondered if he had time for another. He loved the fact that no matter what he ate, it didn't seem to hurt his body much. He was eyeing the counter again when MacManus spoke.

"I have on a black silk shirt and black dress pants. My hair is dark and well; it's very long and loose today. My wife, she likes it down, and I wanted to please her."

Simon nearly snarled at the vampire, but caught himself before he did. He didn't want to give the man reason for not coming at this point. Simon looked at his watch. In about twenty minutes it wouldn't matter anyway. Sara would be his.

"Of course you do. I look forward to seeing you soon then."

After they hung up Simon sat there for several minutes trying to regain control of his temper. Sara was going to be his, not this stupid vampire's. Simon couldn't believe how much it bothered him that his man, this *it*, was thinking he could be a husband to someone like Sara. Simon grinned as he made his way over to the pretzel place again. He was going to have fun making her forget about her husband, not that he thought it would be a problem.

After ordering another triple order of pretzels and also a large Coke, Simon made his way back to his table to eat. He laid his cell phone on the table beside him and waited for the call from David, his wolf from last night.

Kathi S. Barton

CHAPTER 24

"I'm at the bus station now. I have my men at each point watching the wolves that work for Sinclair. Are you sure we can't just kill them now and be done with it?"

Aaron laughed at the man on the cell phone. David Wolff had thought the plan was good to a point, but the thought of the rogue wolves running lose just "curled his tail," he'd told Aaron.

"No. Not yet at any rate. I don't think you told me how you got in so close with Sinclair so quickly. I thought the plan was for you to just become a part of his crew."

David, Bradley's brother and a cop, had volunteered to infiltrate the Sinclair wolf pack and become the ears and eyes for Zane and the others. When he'd contacted his brother at noon to tell him that he'd not only gotten in, but he was now the head wolf in charge, Zane was thrilled. She had been in constant contact with him since they'd shown up at the bus station.

"I just proved to them that I was big man on the premises. Had to kill three of the rogues to do it. After that they pretty much left me alone. Sinclair called me into his office this morning and told me that I was a perfect specimen for what he had in mind. I myself think the man is about half a bun short of a loaf, but then most bad guys are that go up against a badass like yourself."

Aaron laughed again. "Just be safe, my friend, and watch out for Zane. I'm worried for her. She doesn't work well with others and I'm afraid she will take on too much thinking to keep everyone safe."

David agreed.

The plan was simple. Zane would pretend to be Sara and come in through one of the bus terminal doors as though she'd just gotten off the bus. Sara, from the safety of their home, was going to keep the people, mostly humans, in the terminal safe and out of harm's way. Mel was going to be on standby in case Sara needed an extra boost. Zane was going to be "captured" then taken to wherever Sinclair had things set up. They had discovered just yesterday that the lab on the property where Zane had found it wasn't the only lab there was. If they were going to do this they were going to destroy all of them, including the madman at the helm.

Aaron was going to have car trouble and not be able to meet the man at the prearranged place, but have him come and pick Aaron up along the roadside. This was to keep the people at the mall safe as well. Aaron was to keep Sinclair busy until everyone else was in place. While he wasn't thrilled about being a babysitter Aaron was just glad that Sara was safe at home. He wasn't sure where Aiden was in the plan but assumed, like a good mate, he was with Zane.

Aaron moved closer to Sara as they sat on the couch. He laid his hand over her belly and spoke to their child. They had learned with their first two that they could communicate with their unborn through their mental connections. It had proven to be a wonderful experience that they both enjoyed.

"Your mother is going to be a good girl and stay here while daddy goes out and slays the big, bad man for her," he said in a quiet voice.

"And your mother is going to make your daddy sleep in a coffin for real if he doesn't behave himself. Aaron, stop telling this baby nonsense. We both know why I can't leave the house and it had nothing to do with me not being able to take care of myself."

He grinned. "I'm glad you want to keep Mel safe, love, but I can have my fun too. Shamus would kill us if something happened to Mel and I can't say that I blame him. This child, their child, means so much to them and to the magical kingdom."

Mel had been mated to Sherman before, but had no idea that he had manipulated their relationship to make it seem as though she was his. And then when she'd gotten pregnant Sherman had lured her and her guard, one of which was Sara, to the dungeon to kill the guard and also to cause Mel to go into a deep sleep, or Fade, never to return. He had planned to run the kingdom as his own playground. He hadn't expected Sara to survive, nor did he expect her to safeguard Mel until she was strong enough to take him on. It had taken another two years and more magic than they had thought to bring the man to justice. Sherman had been turned into an everlasting tree, always conscious but never able to reach out to anyone for the rest of Mel's life. And Mel, being a true immortal, would never die.

"And as her cousin I can do no less than to protect her, even from herself. She can be a tad headstrong when she thinks she's right." They both looked over at the shimmer of magic just as Mel came into the room.

"You two think you are so funny. Between you and Shamus I can't even come here and watch reruns with Duncan without him making me sign a decree that I won't do anything to make him mad. Everything pisses him off so I don't know how that is supposed to work."

Shamus came into the room through the kitchen with Duncan and the tray of food. "I wouldn't have to worry all the time if you would simply remember that I'm the man of the house and obey my every command." Mel and Sara both snorted.

"Mistress Mel, perhaps you would like to take boxing lessons from me. I was quite the man's man when I was younger. I have moves that would make that chicken man sit up and take notice." Duncan handed Sara a glass of iced tea as he spoke.

"Chicken man, Duncan? I'm afraid…Tyson. Ah, yes, I get it. But I don't believe…never mind. I would have thought that you'd be with me on keeping my Mellie safe, Dunc old man. She is your best friend, isn't she?"

Shamus reached for the chocolate chip cookie that Mel was about to put into her mouth. His hair caught on fire. With the ease of a man who loves a woman with incredible power Shamus simply brushed his hand through his hair and the flames went out. Aaron was no longer concerned that Mel would be harmed today. There was no way anything would get to her with Shamus around. Any man who could be at ease with large, bright red flames shooting off his head while having a mundane conversation with a man who served chocolate chip cookies to a queen could do anything.

"Oh, sire, she is that, but she is also the queen. Her word is all. I would have thought as a mated man, you would have known that. Why, the household here knows that Miss Sara runs this home. She is the backbone and the strength. Master Aaron is just the one who makes her happy and for that, we are very grateful to him."

Aaron wasn't sure if he should be insulted or happy, but his phone ringing stopped the reply he was sure was going to get him into trouble. Zane was on the other end.

"It's time to make your call. Everything is set up. And when you leave the house, make sure that the alpha is close. He will be able to command the wolves quicker than you will."

"All right. Anything else?" He wasn't insulted by her comment as least he tried not to be. He was able to command wolves as well as any other animal thanks to Sara, but he didn't have to like it.

"Yes. Don't get in Aiden's way. If you do, then I'm sure that he will hurt you."

The line went dead. He wasn't sure what that was supposed to mean, but remembered what she said about his guard. They would only protect him as far as he let them and Aiden was the biggest threat to the enemy. Aaron suddenly wondered where Aiden was.

"I must go. Sara, you know the plan. Mel, you two stay here. I need to know that you are both safe before I leave."

A shimmer of magic was all the warning they got before Aiden came into the room. He was…Aaron wasn't sure what it was, but the man radiated power. Aaron looked at Mel and noticed that she, too, was impressed with him.

"I will protect the master, my ladies. He will be with me at all times and I will make sure he does what you have asked. Sire?"

Aaron cocked a brow at Mel. She smiled her answer. "I told him to keep you safe and I would give him a boon. You make sure that I can pay it to him."

Aaron rubbed his hands together. This was going to be fun. And for the first time since Zane had told him what she was planning, he felt as if it was going to work out.

~~~

Zane shifted into Sara's form. It wasn't hard, but awkward. Sara was shorter than Zane and she was smaller boned. Plus, Sara was a girly girl and Zane was not. She stepped through the doors of the terminal just as the wolves, one of them David, stepped in front of her.

"Miss Sara? You need to come with me. There has been an accident at your house and I'm to take you there."

Sara/Zane nodded and walked between the four wolves that walked behind David. When they walked past the restaurant Zane could see Simon getting up and walking toward the exit too. She would not have recognized him without his scent.

He had gotten huge—not only huge, but obese. She would have guessed his weight at around four hundred pounds and this girth had to be at least four feet round. She hadn't caught that when she saw him drive by the mansion. She had a moment to wonder if Aiden wouldn't get squashed by him if he fell.

"You aren't very nice, my love. And I don't plan to let myself get into a position where he is on top of me. I will be standing long after he falls." Aiden chuckled as he answered her query.

"Just don't get too cocky. And don't kill him too quickly. I have to know where the other labs are before he is dead. I think Queen has something planned for him anyway if we don't kill him right away. She is scary when she gets like that."

Zane had met with the queen shortly after she had risen for the day. They had come to an understanding. Not friends, but a sort of truce. The queen was going to grant her wish, a different one this time, if they succeed today. Zane hoped that they would be able to put a stop to this madness once and for all.

"Aaron and I are on the road. We await your call. Be careful. I still owe you an ass beating for leaving my bed this morning."

She didn't tell him where she had gone, only that she had fixed things between her and the queen. The boon the queen was going to give her was just between the two of them. Zane knew it was a lot to ask, but the queen had assured her that she could make it happen.

The van that the wolves put Zane into was a piece of crap, but the windows where dark enough that no one could see what happened inside once the doors were closed. The wolves, all of them wild in the way of the shifter, stupid in other words, were easily duped once they were on the road. David took them to a warehouse just outside the city limits, one that Sara was shielding from the others.

Zane was a little mad. She was spoiling for a good fight and when David had his men come in and subdue them immediately she was disappointed. The rogues were more than willing to lead them to the three labs they knew about and to tell them that there was one more, a big one by all accounts, but they didn't know where it was.

"But you're sure there is one? Have any of you been to it? And if not, then how do you know there is one?" David shook the largest one of the pack and his men stepped forward when they looked ready to fight back.

"That man, Sinclair. He told us if we fucked this up…pardon, ma'am, that we'd be food for them vampires. The wolves, they been feeding them the leftovers when the vamps done eat. Don't want no fucking part…pardon again, ma'am, no f'ing part of that."

Zane tried her best not to laugh. This man was apologizing to her for using the F word and he was willing to kill her when asked to. This really was fucked up. They loaded one of the men into the van again and David took the other three to a holding cell on the pack land. They would be dealt with later.

The first lab was about three miles from the one on Zane's property. There were about eight dead bodies inside and three lab men. It was difficult to figure out just precisely how many dead men there were because their bodies had been cut up into so many pieces. They were told that this lab was the "extraction lab." Here was where they cut up the bodies to see what they could use and not use in the future with the DNA manipulation experiments. Zane killed them all. They were so entrenched in what they were doing they couldn't see what they were doing wrong.

The next lab they were taken to the man in the car wouldn't even get out of the van for. He nearly wet himself when she told him she needed him to go with her.

"Can't. No way. If you make me, then you might as well kill me right now 'cause I'd rather be dead than go in there again. No, nope, nada, no fucking way."

This man didn't apologize for cussing, but he didn't go with her either. She put him into a deep sleep and moved to the building. When she had touched the wolf's mind, she realized that he had come from here and the only reason he'd not been terminated when he failed to perform was because he was willing to kill whatever it took to keep him from being in this lab. The wolf had dreams, nightmares really, every night and probably would for the rest of his life.

Zane moved to just outside the door to the lab and waited for the heat she could feel on the business side of the door to move away. Once it did, she knew that the body on the other side was no longer blocking her from coming in. She couldn't just materialize inside; she didn't know the area and took the chance of coming in on a piece of furniture or worse yet, a person. It was simply easier just to walk in the door. Much more fun too.

The door opened for her as she moved closer to it. She grinned. Whoever was coming out was in for a surprise. As soon as he saw Zane he lifted his rifle and was dead before he got it to his shoulder. His head disintegrated as soon as she removed it. Vampire. Moving into the building she came across three more men, all armed with high powered rifles loaded with silver. She managed to kill them before any alarm could be triggered.

The next set of doors led to a cage area was she found six beings. They were in very bad shape and begged her to end their misery.

Zane had anticipated this and had asked the queen what she wanted done with them. Shamus told her that if she secured the building they would make sure that someone came to help them all. Zane tried to ignore them in hopes of getting them help quickly. She reached out to Shamus and told him what she had found. It took her twenty more minutes to make sure the lab was empty, but she found three more dead bodies up in one of the bedrooms. Each had recently given birth.

"They didn't die of childbirth. Please don't let the queen or Miss Sara know or even come here. It's bad. The babies…if that's what these are, didn't make it either. They are an abomination, sire. Nothing should…keep them away."

"I will, love. I'm sorry you have to see that too. The men and women in the holding cells, can they be moved? I'd like to bring them to the clinic here in this world first then on to the castle infirmary once they are stable."

"They can move. Though I would put them to sleep first." Zane sent Shamus a mental picture of what she had seen in the holding cells. The bedroom upstairs was for her nightmares only.

After assuring her that he'd take care of it she moved out of the building. A crew of beings from the castle showed up within seconds. When she was sure everyone was out, Zane blew it. And like the other building, there would be nothing left in an hour. The flames would burn until the cinder block was nothing more than ash.

The next place was just as bad, bodies in varying stages of death and dismemberment. Zane found two small children, one a pureblooded vampire and the other a pureblooded wolf. A wood nymph and a small pixie were also saved. The pixie was so grateful to be released she demanded to be Zane's bodyguard for the rest of her life. Zane couldn't get rid of the stupid thing.

These beings were also taken to the clinic. The pixie, Sapphire, said she was staying with Zane. Zane was hard pressed not to flick the tiny thing into the medic's pocket and be done with her, but she wouldn't let go of Zane's ear.

"I hope you know that I don't care for you. You will be going back to your homeland as soon as I'm finished with this task."

"We'll see, mistress. I can be of great help to you. I'm a very important person in my realm. You'll see."

The little thing had blue hair that sparkled brightly in the early evening. Her clothes, also blue, were a short skirt with a lacy hem and a t-shirt with a white cat with a red bow in its hair. Her wings, as long as her body, were a lighter blue than her hair, but no less sparkly. They were variegated with as many shades of blue as her namesake. When Sapphire had flown to Zane, her wings gave off a tiny puff of blue magic that signified her task as a pixie. She colored the flowers on the forest floor. Her knee-high boots finished the ensemble.

CHAPTER 25

Aiden was shadowed near Aaron but just visible enough that Danny could see him if he was close enough. The "broken down" car had its hood up and Danny March, Zane's boss, was there with them. Danny had been thrilled to death to help out.

"Is this the monster that Zane is going after? Why, I could probably take him on and come out the winner. Mother pots, he's a big one."

Aiden loved the man's vocabulary when he "cussed." Some of the things that had come from his mouth in the past hour had Aiden holding his sides with laughter. *Mother pots* was just one of many. His favorite, Aiden thought, was "mother Mary, Joseph, and Peter." He didn't know how Peter had fit in with the group, but it still made him laugh. Aaron was warning Danny to stay back.

"I will, I will. Zane said she'd bust my bottom and Russell would do the same if I got so much as a broken fingernail. She is a bossy little thing, isn't she? But I've never seen a woman work on a car like she does. Darn near makes me want to marry the girl just to keep her to myself."

The growl coming from Aiden startled them both. Aaron stiffened, but didn't move. Danny wisely took a step back.

"Just kidding, Aiden. I'm homosexual and right now, I don't think I've ever been happier about that. No, I won't touch what's yours. I know about the territorial nature of mates. I was just kidding."

"I'm sorry. I didn't mean…you have to realize it's not you, it's my nature. I know you won't touch her."

"I'm glad to know that. Yep, more than you know I'm glad to know that."

Sinclair walked up as soon as Aiden faded deeper into the shadows. He looked over the car as though he was going to help out. There wasn't anything they could do to repair the car, not here at any rate. It was one that Zane had been working on and there was neither carbonator nor wires in it. If Sinclair knew anything about cars, he would have noticed it. But apparently, he didn't. Zane whispered through his mind that all was well on her end. She was coming to them.

"I'm P. Simon Sinclair. You must be MacManus."

Aaron had been warned not to touch the man and when Sinclair put his hands out Aaron raised his dirty ones up to show he couldn't take it. The disappointment on his face was profound. Aiden could detect a small silver wire wrapped around Sinclair's wrist and that he had wanted to garrote Aaron with it. Aaron must have sensed the same thing.

"Yes, I'm MacManus. I'm really sorry about this, but I'm going to have to cut this short. My wife, you know. I need to go and get her at the station."

Sinclair laughed. Aaron simply stood up and looked down at the rotund man. They couldn't kill him just yet; they still needed to find the last lab. But playing along with a madman could be tricky.

"Your wife is with me. Well, at my lab. She is mine now, you see, and you and this…" He pointed at Danny. "Human are going to die. It's a shame really, but I've no use for any more vampires. Besides, your kind doesn't last long once we start to cut on them."

Aaron didn't move, didn't even give any indication that he'd heard what Simon had said. He then leaned back against the car and looked at Simon. "Really? That's odd. I don't believe you. Sara is my wife and I don't think she would have anything to do with someone like you. What do you plan to do with her? Bed her? I think not. Sara is used to a man, someone who can satisfy her. You don't even look like you can satisfy yourself."

"What are you doing? Are you nuts? Zane said to go with him, not piss him off. Back off, sire, we need this man." Aiden wanted to pull Aaron back and shake him, but he couldn't without giving himself away.

"Hush. I know what I'm doing. He'll need to prove something to me and I'll get the information we need that way. Listen to me, I've done this before."

"Why, you obnoxious ass. How dare you speak to me like that? You should have more respect for your betters than that. Why, I should—"

"Should what? I'm not impressed with you at all. You are nothing to me or my mate. I want you to leave us alone."

Aiden started to step forward when he felt the first trickle of magic. It wasn't very big at first, but grew exponentially as the seconds ticked by. Before Aiden could step in front of Aaron, a blade was protruding from Aaron's chest and the man was falling to the ground. Seconds later Zane removed Sinclair's head where he stood.

"What the fuck? Get him to the ground. What the hell was he doing taunting the man for. I told him to stand down several times, that he was armed," Zane said as she pulled the blade from Aaron's chest.

"I told him to stop. He said that he could get the information we needed. Stupid, arrogant bastard."

Aaron was speaking. Zane leaned down and listened and then she started cussing. Aiden was startled by how pissed she was.

She looked at Aiden then at Aaron. "I can save him, but his trade is a favor to be asked for later. Is there a…oh I don't know, a list of things to do on your deathbed to piss me off? All right, you fucking bastard, you have your boon, but I'm not sleeping with your ugly old ass. Fuck a duck and watch it waddle, I hate you right now."

Aiden looked down at Aaron and could have sworn that he smiled. Zane moved over Aaron and worked to stop the bleeding. When she was finished Aiden fed the master his blood and then took them all home. Danny was to meet them later with Russell.

Aiden decided that Aaron was as certifiable as the rest of the group.

~~~

Aaron sat on the couch and waited. It wouldn't be long now and Zane and Aiden would be coming to see him. He wanted to rub his hands together in glee, but was worried that the others in the room would think he was up to something which, in this case, he was. Smiling ruefully he thought about the past several days.

Taking a hit to the chest yesterday was foolhardy, he knew this, and Sara reminded him of it every hour on the hour since she found out what he'd done. But he felt that he'd really had no choice. Aiden was going back to Paris and Zane may or may not go with him. Aaron didn't want either of those things to happen. When Duncan came in with his large tray of food and drinks the couple in question walked in behind him.

"Ah, there you are. So glad you could join us. Have a seat. Would you like anything—"

"You didn't give us a choice and I don't want to sit. I want you to get this over with so that I can speak to the queen. She and I have unfinished business to take care of."

Aaron caught the smile before it erupted all over his face. Zane was in for a big surprise if she thought this was the end. He stood when she continued to stand. "I've asked you nicely, Zane. In my house the rules I set down are to be obeyed. Now sit." There was compulsion there, enough to make Aiden sit, but Zane…well, she stood toe to toe with him.

"I'm not your puppy, nor am I yours to rule. I have no connection to you whatsoever. You asked for a boon, though why I should have to honor it is beyond me, and I'm here to pay up as you have demanded. You provoked that man into stabbing you and we both know it."

Aaron had hoped that she wouldn't find that out and resisted the urge to look at his mate. He could feel her anger at him and knew there was going to be hell to pay later. He did, however, glance over at Aiden who stood now right beside his mate.

"Oh, but that's where you're wrong. I do have a connection to you. I have talked with Mel and she had given me the rest of your sentence. I believe I have you for just under another three thousand years."

Aaron felt the surge of anger from Zane. She turned to Mel. Aaron couldn't tell who Zane was mad at more, him or Mel, but he was willing to bet it was close. He didn't flinch when she looked back at him.

"No. No, that's not what...you can't just give away someone as though they are a pair of shoes. I refuse to allow this. I have a favor to receive and you owning me isn't going to—"

"You may ask me your favor," Mel practically purred at her. "Perhaps I'd be willing to grant it. But I won't allow you to no longer be Aiden's mate, nor will I allow you to become a mortal. Other than that, I'll consider it."

Zane stood there trembling with her anger. It had to be that because Aaron could nearly taste it on his tongue and his body was hot from it. She couldn't harm him, not really, but she could do a great deal of damage to those around him and to his home. He didn't so much as blink at her.

"And your boon? I suppose that is something to make me stay here too?"

She was smart, he'd give her that. That's just what the boon was for. "You stay here as my subject." Her snort had him raise a brow at her. "As I was saying, you stay here as my subject and I will grant you the freedom you wish to be separated from Aiden, provided there is no child involved."

When Aiden stepped forward to speak Aaron raised his hand. He knew, hoped, that Aiden would object at her leaving and was glad to see that he'd not been wrong about that.

Zane smiled at him. It wasn't friendly, it wasn't even remotely nice, but just a showing of teeth. He might have been a little frightened if he didn't know his were bigger. He also knew something she didn't.

"You'll let him find himself a more suitable mate?"

Aaron shook his head. He wanted this as clear as crystal. "No. I will release him provided there is no child involved. You have to stay with him as his mate then."

"Accepted. I will—"

"Master, I don't want this. I want her to be with me…I'm in love with her. Zane, please don't do this. I don't care what you've done, what you do. I love you," Aiden begged Zane.

"Aiden, you should have someone more suited to you. Someone without blood on their hands. Hell, I have blood all over my body. I've done things that I've—"

"Do you accept, Allison Zander St. James?" *Please say yes. Please say yes. Please say yes*, Aaron kept saying in his head.

"Yes. I accept. Thank goodness."

"Congratulations."

Aaron sat back down in his chair. He knew it wouldn't take her long to figure this out. Mel had talked to the Fates and had let her use her magic to change the course of Zane's life. It was risky, of course, to go to the Fates for this, but they had been more than willing to help once they heard of all that she had done for the MacManus family and for Mel. It took her less time than he thought.

"Congratulations? For what?" She looked at him for several seconds. Then with a quick look at Aiden she looked back at Aaron. "You can't do that. It's not…what have you done?"

"You're pregnant. And I didn't have a thing to do with you getting that way, just that you could. We have a deal, Allison. Welcome to my Kiss."

Zane swayed and then started to fall. Aiden standing next to her caught her up in his arms and held her to his body. Aaron didn't say a word as the two of them left his office. Sitting down hard himself he took a deep breath and looked at his mate when she spoke up finally.

"You do know that she's not pregnant, right? And when she figures that out she's going to be really pissed at you." Sara smiled as she continued. "And I hope I'm there when she figures it out."

Aaron hoped she was too, he would probably need her help to heal.

"I'm hoping that by the time she figures out that I've lied to her she really will be. Christ, but that was a little intense. She is one stubborn woman. Do you think they're going to have sex right now? That would probably seal the deal if they did."

"I think you should try and think of a better way to use your time than to speculate what one of your…what did you call her? Oh yeah, your subjects is doing. Come to the kitchen, Aaron. Duncan has put the children to bed and I know that he bought all the stuff for me to make a cheeseburger."

Aaron's cock twitched. He loved watching Sara eat and cheeseburgers were the—

"Are there any French Fries?" When she nodded, Aaron picked her up and carried her to the kitchen. It was time he had a little quiet time with his own mate.

Kathi S. Barton